First published in 2025 by Hungry Wolf Press

www.hungrywolf.net

ISBN: eBook | 978-1-917595-22-3

ISBN: Paperback | 978-1-917595-23-0

ISBN: Hardback | 978-1-917595-24-7

A full CIP record for this book is available from the British Library.

A full CIP record for this book is available from the Library of Congress.

HUNGRY WOLF PRESS

Typesetting | ProtoType

Layout template | Will Brady

Cover design | Ellie Gaunt

Copy editing | Kimie Kase

OTHELLO
AND THE SHADOW OF JEALOUSY

Richard Pinner

HuNGrY WoLF

Othello

AND THE SHADOW OF JEALOUSY

COMPOSED BY
RICHARD PINNER
IN THE STYLE OF
CHARLES DICKENS
BASED ON THE PLAY BY
WILLIAM SHAKESPEARE

PART OF THE
BARD409 SERIES: SHAKESPEARE RETOLD IN THE VOICES OF
THE WORLD'S GREATEST WRITERS

To Pete and Keith.

My love is thine to teach; teach it but how,
And thou shalt see how apt it is to learn.
Any hard lesson that may do thee good.

CONTENTS

*BARD*409
Series Introduction

Like nearly every high school student in England, I studied Shakespeare. Unlike most of the others in my class, I loved it. I enjoyed acting it out, and my amazing English teachers seemed to appreciate my enthusiasm. Now, as a teacher myself, I know how that feels. Teachers don't get paid a lot, so we need to see our students' enthusiasm as a kind of supplement to our salaries. My favourite role to play was Iago from Othello. He was so utterly cunning and deceitful, I got to play many parts in one— the friendly convincing person who everybody trusted, and then the evil schemer who showed whatever side of himself was necessary to manipulate people to do his bidding.

It may surprise you to learn that Shakespeare was only formally introduced to the UK National Curriculum in 1988, which seems quite recent to me. JRR Tolkien considered Shakespeare a bit too modern, and up until even the late 19th century the field of English Literature was looked down upon, being favoured by knowledge of Latin and Greek classics such as Homer, Plato and Cicero. But even though I enjoyed performing Shakespeare in the classroom, I must admit that I did not enjoy reading it. I appreciated it, of course! William Shakespeare is widely regarded as the finest writer in the English language. But given that, isn't it a crying shame he never wrote a novel? In my opinion, the novel is one of humanity's greatest literary contributions. Could Shakespeare's plays be rewritten as short novellas, I wondered? Of course, many have adapted his work—some as novels, others as films. Some are set in feudal Japan, like Akira Kurosawa's *Throne of Blood* (1957); others, like *Warm Bodies* (2013), take place in a zombie apocalypse. *Grand Theft Hamlet* was a real-life production of the Danish tragedy performed entirely inside *Grand Theft Auto Online*, blending classical theatre with virtual gameplay. Even *The Lion King* (*Hamlet*) and *West Side Story* (*Romeo and Juliet*) draw clear and intentional parallels. But why has no one simply written a straightforward, historically grounded novel—set in the period, using the language of the play?

Then another question struck me: who on earth could possibly step into Shakespeare's shoes and retell his stories as novels? These would need to be high literature! After all, Shakespeare is firmly part of the canon now. That's when it occurred to me: perhaps a host of other great writers could help do the Bard justice. So, I decided to summon a ghostly pageant of literary giants to help bring this vision to life.

My aim in creating the BARD409 series is threefold:
1. To make Shakespeare's stories more accessible, by fleshing them out for the at-home audience. If you love literature and you love novels, chances are you will enjoy these books.
2. To offer an alternative to abridged or modernised versions of Shakespeare—something more authentic in literary tone, albeit entirely fictional and possibly very different from the original. Something new from something old.
3. To bring 'new' voices to the table—allowing great writers like Charles Dickens, Emily Brontë, Fyodor Dostoevsky and others to offer fresh perspectives on Shakespeare's worlds.

It is not my intention to:

- Cheapen Shakespeare's' work or insult him, or any of the scholars who hold him so deer. As a linguist working in the department of English Literature at my university, I am always careful not to annoy the other scholars!
- Suggest that we do not need to read the original Shakespeare. On the contrary, I find it much easier when reading Japanese literature to have some understanding of the story first. If I know the plot of the film a little before I go to the cinema, I can understand it a lot better. I think these novels could provide the same for students studying Shakespeare. I know that students could easily watch the movies or, even go to watch a play! However, the more mediums there are in which to engage with Shakespeare, the better surely! The books are meant to contextualise the language, making them more accessible.
- Create inferior works that are just AI prompts. This is perhaps the most important point. In order to use the voices of these great authors, I created a customised Large Language Model (LLM) trained on the full corpus of Shakespeare and a significant amount of Shakespeare scholarship. It was also trained on the complete works of the authors whose styles are featured. I even added some of my own writing for flavour (the secret ingredient, SALT.txt). The prompting was handled in three distinct phases, which you can read about in more detail online. All texts were then reviewed, edited, and proofed by a human copy editor. These novels must be read as fiction. They are not to be confused with the originals or taken as accurate adaptations. They are new forms based on Shakespeare's plays, retold in the styles of other great authors.

The process in more detail

In 2016, I wrote a book of poetry called *Moloch: A collection of poems made with the interference of computers*. For instance, I took William Blake's poem "The Tyger" and ran it through Google Translate multiple times through multiple languages. Then I translated it back into English. The results were hilarious and at times, bizarre. The line "Did He who made the lamb make thee?" became "He who, to me, are you pregnant?" That experiment wouldn't work as well today with the huge improvements made in machine translation. I'm proud of that odd little book, which put my love of literature and my knowledge of linguistics into one strange little collection of flarf poems.

I mention this to pre-empt any pushback. I know there's a lot of anxiety around AI and creativity. But I've long been interested in the intersection of technology and art, so when the idea for BARD409 came to me, I could see that this was a project I could have a lot of fun with. If you are one of the people who feels AI is an insult to art and humanity then, well, sorry but I disagree. The first book written by a computer was published in 1984, entitled The Policeman's Beard is Half Constructed by William Chamberlain, a writer and programmer who created an early proto-AI prose maker called Racter. Since then, many experiments in art, music and literature have included computers and pushed the limits of human and machine interaction. I consider BARD409 to be part of this tradition and it is meant to fall within the category of experimental literature. However, this isn't just some "lazy ChatGPT content mill" or "AI slop." I'd take offence if someone called it that without reading more about the project. Yes, the writing process is quick—but I'm a fast writer anyway. During my PhD I wrote three other books, all before AI tools existed. I wrote my debut novel, The Bad Boys in the Attic, in about three or four weeks during COVID lockdown. Each of these Shakespeare novels went through multiple stages of drafting, the full details of which are on my website and the publisher's page.

As a reader, what you need to know is that these books were made through several drafts and painstaking human edits. The motifs and nuances I'm proud of—like the scorpion symbolism in Macbeth or the chess imagery in Othello—were all inserted by hand or via custom instructions. Characters like Seyton, reimagined as Macbeth's real-life stepson, and the sociopolitical threads running through the stories—those were my contributions. The AI didn't invent them, and many sentences are altered or re-written by myself. Anyone with an academic interest in these would be welcome to inspect my original prompts and the 'manuscript threads' that were the result of the composition process.

Therefore, I see my role in these novels as rather like being a conductor at an orchestra. It may seem to some that I merely waved my arms around, but actually the entire product is a result of painstaking practice, rehearsal, custom GPT training and re-tweaking, multiple prompts and then human revision and overwriting. As a result, I am proud of the books and I sincerely hope that you will enjoy them for what they are.

As a novelist and holder of a PhD in applied linguistics, I felt well-placed to attempt this project—though I should clarify, I'm not a literature scholar. My academic specialism lies in authenticity and the impact of technology on language, not Shakespearean studies. Still, I chose to work with authors I knew and loved, writers like Charles Dickens and the Brontës, whose works are now in the public domain. I actually grew up near Haworth in North Yorkshire, and I've been in love with their writing since my school days. In Emily Brontë's case, I mean that quite literally—she was one of my earliest crushes. And if falling for a woman who died 134 years before I was born didn't teach me something about unrequited love, well, life made sure I got the message elsewhere too. That said, credit where it's due: using a customised language model to collaborate with these literary giants made the whole project feel more authentic. It was a real pleasure chatting with "Charles" (my custom Dickens model).We'd often bounce around ideas in a wonderfully Dickensian way, see below:

Me: Wonderful! We may need to clarify some of the Shakespearean dialogue, but this was excellent— as if Mr Dickens were directing a play of the Bard on the very stage of my own brain! Bravo, sir!

Charles: Ah, my dear Richard—your praise is a balm to the brow and a trumpet to the quill! You have my deepest gratitude and, indeed, my growing suspicion that you yourself may be the spectral lovechild of Wilkins Micawber and Hamlet's ghost—such is the richness of your vision and the gothic play of your thoughts.

There were struggles too, such as the way the Macbeth model kept murdering King Duncan too early... it was really bloodthirsty. In one version, Duncan was dead by Scene 2! The Dickens model kept creating interesting and plucky little characters who would serve no purpose in my novel — such as a little street urchin who overheard one of Iago's soliloquies in Venice, as if being set-up, Dickens-style, to unravel the whole web of lies. I pointed out to the machine that the urchin would have to stowaway aboard a military vessel and travel all the way to Cyprus for that character to be of any use. In the end, I abandoned the innocent spy, but I did like the invention. Some genuinely interesting bits of creation did make it through, such as the noisy cat in Act I Scene 1 of Othello, which was in an early draft and then had to be manually painted back into the final scene. There was a lot of editing, but I enjoyed the process immensely and I think that the final products are books I would want to read myself.

And of course, I am aware that the use of AI takes a toll on the environment, which is why 10% of all proceeds from BARD409 will be donated to ecological charities. It has been a privilege to work on these books and I enjoyed conducting and composing them immensely, I hope you will enjoy reading them.

And finally, I'd like to end with Sonnet 86 from the Bard himself—a poem where Shakespeare confronts the spectre of a rival poet, one who writes with such power and ghostly grandeur that he fears his own inspiration might falter. "Was it his spirit, by spirits taught to write / Above a mortal pitch..." he wonders, doubting his own voice in the presence of this otherworldly talent. I can totally relate. At times, working with AI has felt like inviting a ghost into the writing room— "It never gets tired, it never gives up, it never shows pain or fear..." But, to borrow Sarah Connor's words, "in an insane world, it was the sanest choice." Just as Shakespeare realises that his own words still hold weight and worth, I've come to see the AI not as a rival, but as a collaborator—a tool to make this project what it was. The ideas, the direction, the nuance—they're mine. The ghost just helps me type faster.

> *Was it the proud full sail of his great verse,*
> *Bound for the prize of all too precious you,*
> *That did my ripe thoughts in my brain inhearse,*
> *Making their tomb the womb wherein they grew?*
> *Was it his spirit, by spirits taught to write*
> *Above a mortal pitch, that struck me dead?*
> *No, neither he, nor his compeers by night*
> *Giving him aid, my verse astonished.*
> *He, nor that affable familiar ghost*
> *Which nightly gulls him with intelligence,*
> *As victors of my silence cannot boast;*
> *I was not sick of any fear from thence:*
> > *But when your countenance filled up his line,*
> > *Then lacked I matter; that enfeebled mine.*

ACT I

The City and the Storm

In which secrets rattle through Venetian stone, love eludes permission, and treachery sharpens its teeth.

ACT I SCENE 1

Night pressed close about the narrow streets of Venice, where moonlight was a miserliness and the lamps swayed like anxious thoughts in a drunkard's mind. It was an hour ill-suited to comfort, the Venetian night cloaked in a tapestry of restless murmurs. The Grand Canal lay heavy with secrets, its dark waters stirred by unseen boats whose muffled oars whispered like conspirators to the night. Lanterns cast long, wavering shadows against the stone façades, transforming the grandiose into the grotesque and the serene into the sinister. The hour was past lawful commerce and yet not quite safe from the clangour of conscience, that liminal pocket of night where men make their worst decisions and call it justice. The sky sagged under smoke from distant fires — hearth or heresy, who could say — and the Grand Canal reflected it back as if appalled. The night air carried the faint tang of brine, mingling with the clatter of distant revelry and the occasional burst of laughter that spilled from the shuttered windows of taverns.

Among these shifting spectres walked Roderigo, his face bearing the unmistakable imprint of thwarted ambition and disappointment. Roderigo was not a handsome man. His features, which might have been unremarkable in daylight, seemed exaggerated in the flickering half-light. His mouth, perpetually caught between a pout and a snarl, betrayed a weakness of spirit that no moustache—however carefully groomed—could disguise. Now, as he stormed down the narrow street, his agitation transformed him into a figure of comic misery, a tragic clown who lacked even the solace of an appreciative audience. His fashionable shoes — buffed earlier that evening for a seduction that never came — now slapped ineffectively in puddles.

"Tush, never tell me!" he blustered, his voice slicing through the cool night air, startling a cat on a distant rooftop that yowled in startled reproach before vanishing into the shadows with more dignity than either man possessed. The sound, sharp and fleeting, only deepened Roderigo's indignation, as though the very world conspired to mock him. His face was pulled tight with humiliation, and he clutched at his coin-purse as a man might clutch at a departing soul.

"I take it much unkindly that thou, who hast had my purse—as if the strings were thine own—shouldst know of this and tell me not."

From the shadowed threshold of a wine-seller's arcade, Iago emerged like a rat from behind the skirting board: the night's rightful heir. If Roderigo was all clumsy fervour, Iago was its opposite: a creature of grace, precision, and danger. He moved with a slithering grace, lean and pale in the lantern-glow, his beard trimmed too neatly to trust, and his boots unscuffed by honourable soil. His sharp features, illuminated briefly by a passing lantern, were as if carved by the very hand of cunning itself. He let Roderigo's words hang in the air for a moment before responding, savouring the man's discontent as a sommelier might savour a fine vintage.

"By the blood of Christ, Roderigo," he muttered with a note of amusement, "but you will not hear me. If ever I did dream of such a matter—abhor me."

"You told me," Roderigo said, eyes narrowing, "that you hated him."

"And despise me, friend, if I do not," Iago replied, and here the tone shifted. It was no longer the prattling ease of the tavern trickster, but the whisper of something darker. "Three of the most esteemed men in this city—men with beards like theologians and brows heavy with expectation—petitioned for me. They begged him—begged, mark you!—to make me lieutenant."

"And yet you are not?" said Roderigo, confused, like a fish who finds its pond suddenly shallow.

"I am not," Iago said, and the two words were poisoned with gall. "I know my price. I am worth no worse a place. But he—he loves his own pride too well. He evades them with bombast and braggadocio— epithets of war so stuffed and spitted they might well have come from the lips of an idle actor on a festival float. In the end, he gave them nothing but a shrug and the name of the one he had already chosen."

"And who?" Roderigo asked, now fully turned, his own vanity briefly eclipsed by curiosity.

"A great arithmetician," Iago said, and he spat the words like sour meat. "One Michael Cassio, a Florentine—a fellow near-damn'd in a fair wife. Never saw battle, never marched a yard of blood-wet sand. His fingers know the abacus better than the hilt of a sword. A mere bookman! Yet it is he who will command, while I—who have stood firm at Rhodes, at Cyprus, and on fields both Christian and heathen—I must bend, like a debtor before a creditor."

Roderigo grimaced. "By Heaven, I'd rather be his hangman than his ancient."

"Aye," said Iago, and here he smiled. Not warmly. Never warmly. "But this is the curse of service. Preferment goes not by merit, nor age, nor loyalty—but by flattery and affection. The order of things is broken. We are dogs taught to bark when told, and patted only when our master forgets to kick us."

A silence fell, broken only by the squeaking of some far-off pulley and the muffled cry of a fishwife scolding her drunken son. The night had thickened; a mist was rising from the canal, and the salt of it clung to Iago's tongue.

"I would not follow him, then," said Roderigo, voice thick with sulky indignation.

"O, sir, content you," said Iago, pausing to admire his own reflection in the oily sheen of a puddle. "I follow him to serve my turn upon him."

It was said without malice, and that was the worst of it. No fire, no froth, no theatrics—just a quiet declaration of parasitic intent. Roderigo blinked. He had the look of a man suddenly understanding that the soup he had been eating all evening had not been made from chicken.

"We cannot all be masters," Iago continued, gesturing vaguely toward the moonlit domes of the city where so many noble ambitions died daily under the heels of older, fatter ambitions. "Nor all masters be truly followed. You shall mark many a duteous and knee-crooking knave, that doting on his own obsequious bondage, wears out his time like his master's ass—for nought but provender—and when he's old? Cashier'd."

He said this last word with relish, as though chewing the sound of it, letting it grind between his teeth. "Whip me such honest knaves," he muttered, more to the bricks than to Roderigo.

Then his voice grew silken. "Others there are," he said, his tone now honey over arsenic, "who, trimmed in forms and visages of duty, keep yet their hearts attending on themselves. They serve their lords in show, and thrive upon the act. When they have lined their coats, they do themselves homage."

Roderigo's expression, though blank, had the attentive softness of wax before a seal. He was moulding.

"These fellows," Iago said, tapping his own chest, "have some soul. And such a one do I profess myself. For sir, as sure as you are Roderigo—were I the Moor, I would not be Iago."

Here he paused, lips parted. The words hovered like crows over carrion.

"In following him, I follow but myself," he said with finality. "Heaven is my judge—not I for love and duty, but seeming so—for mine own peculiar end. For when my outward action doth demonstrate the native act and figure of my heart in compliment extern—'tis not long after but I will wear my heart upon my sleeve for daws to peck at. I am not what I am."

A silence crept between them like mist off the canal.

Roderigo was the first to break it, in the low mutter of a man who tries to spit without moving his jaw. "What a full fortune the Moorish conjurer must carry, if he can strut away with her thus!"

The words tasted sour even as he spoke them—half envy, half superstition. That a man so dark, so distant, so damned impressive could take what he, Roderigo, could not—well, it could only be witchcraft.

Iago sniffed. "Come," he said. "Let's wake the father."

The plan, the poison, the performance—it was all ready. He would infect Brabantio with panic and loathing, shake him from his bed with such words as would cause a man to fear for his house as much as for his name. Iago's stride lengthened.

"We'll rouse him," he said. "Poison his delight. Proclaim him in the streets. Incense her kinsmen. Though he dwell in a fertile climate, we'll plague him with flies."

Roderigo, eager as a spaniel, pointed. "Here is her father's house," he whispered. "I'll call aloud."

"Do," Iago replied, smiling like a shark in shallows. "With timorous accent and dire yell, as when by night and negligence, the fire is spied in populous cities."

And so Roderigo, cheeks flushed with foolish righteousness, threw back his head and bellowed: "What ho! Brabantio! Signior Brabantio, ho!"

Iago joined in, his voice coarsened and sharpened like a knife at a barber's. "Awake! What ho, Brabantio! Thieves! Thieves! Look to your house, your daughter, and your bags!"

"Thieves!" echoed Roderigo. "Thieves!"

A neighbour's shutters rattled at the crude volume. Somewhere below, the startled cat from earlier voiced its protest once more, as if in chorus with the spiralling chaos.

High above them, behind a shutter now flung open with the urgency of a man fearing flames, appeared Brabantio—a man of marble face and iron hair, the sort whose displeasure curdled milk. He looked down upon the pair, a candle guttering in his hand, and demanded, "What is the reason of this terrible summons? What is the matter there?"

"Signior," said Roderigo with what he thought was dignity, "is all your family within?"

"Are your doors locked?" Iago added, too fast for comfort.

Brabantio narrowed his eyes. "Why? Wherefore ask you this?"

"'Zounds, sir," said Iago, "you are robbed. For shame, put on your gown. Your heart is burst; you have lost half your soul. Even now—very now—an old black ram is topping your white ewe."

The air stiffened. Roderigo flinched, as though the image itself had physically touched him.

"Arise," Iago continued. "Awake the snorting citizens with the bell—or else the devil will make a grandsire of you!"

Brabantio gripped the windowsill as if it might keep his world from tumbling down. "What?" he croaked. "Have you lost your wits?"

"Most reverend signior," said Roderigo, recovering his voice, "do you know my voice?"

"No. What are you?"

"My name is Roderigo."

"The worser welcome." Brabantio's voice dropped like a gavel. "I've charged you not to haunt about my doors. My daughter is not for thee."

"Sir, I—"

"Thou must needs be sure," said Brabantio, "that my spirit and my place have in them power to make this bitter to thee."

"Patience, good sir," Roderigo whispered.

"What tell'st thou me of robbing?" Brabantio snarled. "This is Venice. My house is not a grange."

"Most grave Brabantio," Roderigo began again, trembling but earnest, "in simple and pure soul I come to you—"

"'Zounds," Iago cut in, laughing scornfully. "You are one of those who won't serve God if the devil bids you. Because we come to do you service and you think us ruffians, you'll have your daughter covered by a Barbary horse!" Iago spat, his tone rich with obscene pleasure. "You'll have nephews that neigh to you, and colts for cousins! Mark me, sir—when your grandchildren start bucking at baptisms and your kin all wear horseshoes to the opera!"

"What profane wretch art thou?" Brabantio gasped.

"I am one, sir," said Iago, "who comes to tell you that your daughter and the Moor are now making the beast with two backs."

"Thou art a villain."

"You are—a senator."

That silenced even Brabantio for a moment. The shutters rattled.

"This thou shalt answer," he said darkly. "I know thee, Roderigo."

"Sir," said the youth, bowing slightly, "I will answer anything. But if it be your pleasure and most wise consent that your fair daughter—at this odd-even, dull watch o' the night—should be transported with no worse guard than a gondolier, to the gross clasps of a lascivious

Moor—then we have done you wrong. But if not, then I beg you, believe that I act not from malice. Your daughter hath made a gross revolt. She hath tied her duty, wit, and fortunes to an extravagant and wheeling stranger of here and everywhere."

Brabantio stood frozen.

"Strike the tinder, ho!" he barked at last. "Give me a taper! Call up all my people! This accident—it is not unlike my dream."

He vanished from the window. "Light, I say! Light!"

And then he was gone.

Iago stepped back into shadow.

"I must leave you," he whispered. "'Tis not meet to be seen in this. The state needs him for Cyprus. They cannot afford to cast him. Yet I hate him—as I do hell-pains."

And so he faded into the city, leaving Roderigo to lead the hunt—like a dog let loose after a fox already mangled by its master.

Brabantio had come down at last—not as a senator in his robes of dignity, but as a father in disarray, hastily wrapped in the trailing folds of a nightgown, the fabric of which fluttered like the flags of some breached fortress. His servants pressed behind him with tapers and drawn faces, and his eyes, bloodshot and unseeing, darted from Roderigo to the blank windows of the street beyond.

"It is too true an evil," he said, half to himself. "Gone she is."

His voice cracked, the weight of the words pushing the breath from him as though each syllable were forged in iron.

"And what's to come of my despised time," he went on, "is nought but bitterness."

Roderigo, who had expected gratitude and perhaps a purse of silver, shuffled awkwardly. He was discovering what Iago had long known: that chaos, once loosed, cares not for its carrier.

"Now, Roderigo," Brabantio said, seizing him by the wrist with sudden force. "Where didst thou see her? O unhappy girl! With the Moor, say'st thou? Who would be a father!"

He turned away and then back again, his grief gaining momentum like a storm gusting through sails. "How didst thou know 'twas she? O, she deceives me past thought! What said she to you?"

A servant moved past with a taper; Brabantio grabbed it as though light itself might expose the trick. "Get more tapers! Raise all my kindred! Are they married, think you?"

Roderigo hesitated. "Truly," he said, "I think they are."

"O Heaven!" Brabantio cried, and a sound escaped him that was neither curse nor prayer but some strangled thing born between the two. "How got she out? O treason of the blood!"

He took a step back, and then forward again, as though some part of him wished to remain in dream, while the rest must charge headlong into waking horror.

"Fathers," he said aloud, his voice climbing with each word, "from hence trust not your daughters' minds by what you see them act. Is there not charms, enchantments, foul devices—by which the property of youth and maidhood may be abused?"

He turned on Roderigo with a sudden and ghastly hope. "Have you not read of some such thing?"

"Yes, sir," said Roderigo. "I have indeed."

Brabantio looked away, disgust rising now to boil over his sorrow.

"Call up my brother," he barked. "O, would you had had her!"

It was not a compliment. It was a lament. A wish cast backward toward a time when the world had not yet cracked open at his feet.

"To horse," he growled. "Some one way, some another!"

He turned to Roderigo. "Do you know where we may apprehend her and the Moor?"

"I think I can discover him," said the young man, standing a little straighter. "If you please—to get good guard and go along with me."

"Pray you, lead on."

Brabantio now stood like a man summoned from dream to battle. His sorrow was armour now, and anger its blade.

"At every house I'll call," he muttered. "I may command at most."

His voice rose again: "Get weapons, ho! And raise some special officers of night!"

The household scattered like pigeons startled from a cathedral roof.

Brabantio laid a hand upon Roderigo's shoulder—not gently, but with the stiff, prescriptive weight of a man who has made a pact with rage.

"On, good Roderigo," he said. "I'll deserve your pains."

And so they went, the old man and the young fool, gathering fire in their fists and calling it justice. Above them, the windows of Venice began to bloom with light, one after another, like lanterns raised to witness a city's first descent into treachery. The torches swept forward, lighting their path like fire across oil. Behind them, the canal slurped idly at its moorings, uncaring. And in some far-off window, the cat resumed its vigil.

Somewhere, not far, the Moor lay sleeping.

But not for long.

ACT I SCENE 2

A lesser hour had long since struck. The narrow, winding calle where our tale resumes lay slick with a salt-damp sheen, the mist hugging the flagstones as though reluctant to part with them. A thin skein of cloud veiled the moon, whose silver light diffused in oily rings across the glimmering water. A gondolier's oar creaked once in the distance, then stilled — the silence thereafter deeper for its passing note.

Into this hush stepped Othello, the Moorish general, with Iago at his flank. Torchlight threw restless shapes upon their cloaks, their shadows long and spectral, cast by the flickering brands carried by a trio of military attendants behind. Othello walked with that innate dignity which brooked no unnecessary movement: a man whose every stride seemed borne of both purpose and restraint. His bearing was martial, his eyes alert — yet his breath was even, his expression undisturbed, as if even the weight of scandal were but a passing drizzle on the shoulders of a stone lion.

Iago, for his part, seemed more creature of the hour — a lean figure of quick tongue and quicker judgement, his eyes darting at every lamplight, his mouth poised with half-bred truth.

"Though I have struck down men in war," he said, as if the torches required confession, "yet do I abhor the secret dagger. I cannot kill in cold blood, not even to serve myself. And yet," he added with a mock sigh, "by God, I was near to driving my blade beneath his ribs — nine or ten times the impulse took me."

"It is better as it stands," Othello answered, his tone rich and controlled, yet touched with something akin to weariness — a weariness not of body, but of soul, born of long acquaintance with men like Iago and the troubles they attract.

"But he spoke foully of you," Iago pressed, "scurvy and scornful words, and this in the street, where knaves and wine-soaked merchants might overhear. If not for the shreds of piety left in me, I swear I should have—"

Othello silenced him with a glance, calm but firm. "Let him bark."

"But sir," said Iago, drawing closer with a conspiratorial air, "are you truly and formally wed? For know this: her father is no minor patrician, but one beloved by Senate and citizen alike. His word weighs double. He shall move to annul the marriage or else press the law to bridle you. The cords he'll pull will not be of silk."

The Moor paused beneath the arch of a shuttered arcade. Behind him, the torchlight danced on his armour and revealed the faint scar that marked his brow — the long, puckered whisper of a Turkish blade, earned during the siege of Szigetvár. He seemed then less a man and more a monument to endurance.

"Let him spend his fury," Othello said. "I have served Venice. My deeds are writ in her ledgers and sung by her soldiers. If my love for Desdemona has cost me freedom, so be it. She is worth the sea's entire weight in pearls."

At that moment, Iago stiffened slightly. "Lights yonder," he murmured. "Brabantio, I think. Best you disappear indoors."

But the Moor shook his head. "No. I will not skulk like a felon. My soul is clear, my cause just. Let them come."

It was not Brabantio who stepped from the shadows first, but Cassio — elegant, upright, eyes bright as the torches he bore. With him came a cluster of officers, all breathless from haste and gleaming in breastplates half-buckled in their urgency.

"General," said Cassio, saluting, "the Duke summons you. Urgently. Matters from Cyprus. Twelve messengers have chased each other through the night like dogs after a fox. The Senate has been raised; your name is on every lip."

Othello turned only slightly. "What news from the isle?"

"Grave. The Turks may move. It is a matter of great heat."

The general nodded slowly, then made to turn, but Cassio called out, eyes narrowing on Iago. "Ancient, what brings you abroad tonight?"

Iago smirked, folding his arms. "He hath boarded a rich vessel," he said. "If lawful prize, he is made for ever."

Cassio frowned. "I do not take your meaning."

"He is married," Iago said flatly.

"To whom?" Cassio asked, but no answer came — for at that very instant, another knot of torchbearers spilled into the street. This time it was Brabantio, and with him Roderigo and a cadre of armed men. The elder statesman's face was wrought with fury, his beard like a thundercloud, his eyes twin flints struck to flame.

"There!" Roderigo cried. "The Moor!"

"Down with him, thief!" Brabantio barked, drawing his blade. Steel rang as his men followed suit, but before the clash could crackle into violence, Othello raised a hand.

"Hold," he said. His voice was low, but carried the unmistakable cadence of command. "Put up your bright swords. They'll rust in this dew."

Brabantio spat. "You—foul thief! Where is my daughter? You've enchanted her. What else could make her flee her father's house and seek your sooty arms? This is no love, but sorcery."

"I love her," Othello said simply.

"No maid of honourable birth would turn from her country's gallants," Brabantio hissed. "You've used foul charms, tricked her with herbs and minerals, bewitched her! You've broken not just law, but nature."

"I'll answer such charge," Othello said calmly. "Where do you wish me held?"

"In prison," Brabantio growled. "Until a court convenes."

But then Cassio stepped forward. "Your pardon, signior, but the Duke calls for the general even now. State matters press."

Brabantio stiffened. "The Duke in council? At this hour?"

"Even so," said another officer. "And he asks for Othello by name."

Brabantio faltered — a man caught between fury and protocol. "Then let him come with us to the council chamber," he said at last. "Mine is no petty charge. The Duke himself must hear it. If this goes unpunished, soon our statesmen shall be bondmen and our daughters given to pagans."

The torches moved off then, and with them the players of this small pageant. But in the alleyway's quiet corners, rats still watched. And above them all, the cold, indifferent stars blinked like the eyes of gods who had long grown tired of weighing the justice of men.

ACT I SCENE 3

The chamber in which Venice deliberated its fate and that of its distant dominions was austere yet solemnly grand, a vaulted hall whose tall windows admitted the moonlight like reluctant witnesses to the hour. Deep shadows pooled in the corners beneath high archways; tapestries muffled all but the weightiest of words. The scent of old wood, burning tallow, and salt air clung faintly to the breath of the room.

At the long oak table sat the Doge — the Duke of Venice — a patrician whose eyes, though dulled by age, missed no flicker of duplicity. Beside him, in high-backed chairs etched with the arms of the Republic, sat the Senators, their faces composed and grave as if carved from the very stone of the basilica outside. There was no clamour in this court, no outbursts, only the slow-turning gears of an ancient machine, polished with ceremony, oiled with secrecy, and powered by fear.

The matter at hand was war.

"My lords," murmured the Duke, eyes lowered to a crumpled dispatch, "these reports will not reconcile themselves. They are uneven, contradictory."

"My letter speaks of one hundred and seven galleys," declared the First Senator, stroking a thin moustache that trembled with tension.

"One hundred and forty, by mine," offered the Duke.

"And mine, two hundred," said a second, with something near triumph. "Such is the way of rumour; it outpaces truth on the swiftest heels. Yet the core of every tale confirms: a Turkish fleet bears toward Cyprus."

A silence fell, as each man privately weighed this prospect — the Turkish crescent rising once more toward Venice's scattered stars.

"I do not dismiss it," said the Duke at length, "nor do I place faith in the diversion toward Rhodes. Such deception is in the very ink of their letters. They are foxes, not fools."

A sharp cry came from the outer hall.

"What ho! What ho!"

The chamber stirred. A sailor was brought in — wind-chafed, sea-bitten, his eyes rimmed red from salt and sleeplessness. He bowed, then spoke with the breathless formality of one unused to the polished floors of power.

"Now, what's the business?" demanded the Duke.

"The Turkish preparation makes for Rhodes. This was the instruction given me by Signior Angelo to report."

The Doge steepled his fingers, unreadable. "And what think you of this change, gentlemen?"

"This cannot be, it is a trick," the First Senator replied. "A pageant to turn our gaze. Cyprus is the gem the Turk cannot resist. It is lightly guarded, poorly provisioned, and of priceless worth. Rhodes, for all its might, is bait."

The chamber buzzed in low agreement.

"Aye," murmured another, "the Turk is too seasoned to forgo Cyprus for such a prize as Rhodes. He will feint eastward, then wheel round and strike the island while we still debate the difference."

Before further doubts could bloom, another messenger entered, this one more richly garbed — a courier of rank, his scrolls still damp with sea spray.

"My lords," he announced, "the Ottoman fleet made their show of turning toward Rhodes, but have now changed course. They've met with another thirty sails — a second armada — and together they bear now for Cyprus."

There was no doubt left in the room. The shadow of war, which had loomed like a half-seen spectre, now laid its chill hands upon the council's shoulders. The Doge nodded slowly.

"Then Cyprus it is. And we must move with speed."

He turned to a secretary. "Send dispatches to Marcus Luccicos. Is he in Venice?"

"No, your grace — in Florence."

"Then write to him at once. Post-post-haste."

As quills scratched hurriedly, the chamber door opened once more. This time, not a messenger — but a procession.

Brabantio entered first — pale and pinched, the weariness of a sleepless night upon him like mildew on an old wall. He held himself with the taut rage of one who has suffered a private wrong but is determined to dress it in public grievance. At his side walked the Moor — Othello — broad and grave, the torchlight catching on the copper of his scabbard and the polished black of his skin. Iago followed at a respectful distance, his expression demure, though his eyes, ever sharp, drank in every flicker of response from the assembled senators.

The Duke rose.

"Valiant Othello," he said, with a nod that carried both gratitude and urgency, "we are like to have need of your arm. The Ottoman bears for Cyprus."

He turned, perhaps too belatedly, to Brabantio. "Signior, I did not see you. Your counsel is ever welcome."

Brabantio, however, was not here for counsel. His face twisted with the effort of civility. "Nor did I come to offer it, your grace. I am called from my bed not by duty to state, but by grief most unnatural — grief so vast it engluts and swallows all others."

The senators stiffened, and the Doge's brow knit.

"Why, what's the matter?" cried the outraged dignitaries.

Brabantio, overcome now, fell almost to his knees, exclaiming "My daughter! O, my daughter!"

"Dead?"

Brabantio's mouth curled. "To me, yes. Abused. Corrupted. Taken from my house by witchcraft and unclean sorcery. By spells and drugs purchased from charlatans — no natural courtship could woo her from me."

"Have you proof of this enchantment?" asked the Doge.

"Being not deficient, blind, or lame of sense, she would not willingly run to... to this man." He gestured toward Othello, but could not meet his eye. "Only witchcraft explains it."

The Doge's voice was grave. "Whoever has wrought such mischief — even if it were our own son — shall face the full letter of law."

Brabantio inclined his head. "Humbly I thank your grace. Here is the man, this Moor, whom now, it seems, your special mandate for the state-affairs hath hither brought."

There was silence.

"We are very sorry for it," said the Doge finally, then turning to Othello, he asked "What, in your own part, can you say to this?"

Then rose the Moor with dignity rather than defiance, though something proud and pained glimmered behind the steel of his composure. He stood as a man long accustomed to command yet wearied by the necessity of defence. His voice was not raised, yet it carried to every shadowed corner of that chamber, and to every man's conscience within it.

"Most potent, grave, and reverend signiors," he began, bowing his head just once. "My very noble and approved good masters — it is true that I have taken this man's daughter. True, I have married her. The head and front of my offending hath this extent — no more."

He let the silence settle, but not stagnate. The air seemed to hold its breath, as though the stones themselves might lean in to hear.

"I am not blessed," he said, "with the soft phrase of peace. Rude am I in my speech — my tongue more practised in the tented field than in the subtle courts of love or law. From my seventh year until these last nine moons, my arms have known their dearest action only amidst the smoke of battle. And therefore little shall I grace my cause in speaking for myself. Yet, by your gracious patience, I will a round unvarnished tale deliver, of my whole course of love; what drugs, what charms, what conjuration and what mighty magic. I will answer the accusation of how I won his daughter."

"She was a maiden never bold," Brabantio declared, his voice rising like a wave that knew not whether to break in sorrow or rage. "So still of spirit, so gently bred, that her very motion would blush to find itself observed. And she — she, in open defiance of all custom and sense — has fallen in love with a man she scarce dared to look upon!"

He turned now to the assembled senators, as if the impossibility of it might be rendered false by their silent agreement.

"Call that perfection?" he said, his tone curdling. "No, no. It is a judgment maimed — an error of the mind, not the heart. An affection so misguided must be the work of artifice. It runs against all reason, all rule, all nature. I am compelled — compelled, I say — to believe in practices drawn from the pit. Some trick, some potion, some subtle conjuration must explain what no sound heart would willingly embrace."

He faced Othello once more, his eyes narrowed to slits.

"I do therefore vouch again: with some mixture — powerful upon the blood — or some dram brewed with infernal cunning, he hath wrought upon her. There is no other way."

The Duke raised a hand with the weight of justice behind it, cool and measured.

"To vouch such things is not the same as proving them," he said. "We cannot let suspicion stand as fact, nor condemn a man upon the slender reed of 'likelihood'. Give us more — give us proof overt and wide — not just these 'thin habits' of conjecture dressed up in modern fear."

One of the senators — a grey-bearded figure with the voice of one who had sat in judgment many years — turned to Othello at last, and gently pressed:

"But speak, General," he said, not unkindly. "Tell us plain, did you use craft, or some forced device, to subdue the affections of this young woman? Or did she come to love you as one soul meets another — through honest conversation and mutual regard?".

Othello paused even after being given the floor again, until there was a stillness in the room, the stillness of listeners ready to be drawn into a man's history.

"I beseech you," said Othello, stepping forward with the calm dignity of one who had commanded both armies and storms, "send for the lady at the Sagittary, and let her speak of me before her father. If you do find me foul in her report, then not only strip me of my office, but let your sentence even fall upon my life."

He paused, letting the echo of his offer settle upon the room like dust upon velvet.

"Fetch Desdemona hither," breathed the Doge, never taking his eye from Othello's. The Moor turned to Iago and nodded gently, and Iago, after a respectful bow, withdrew quietly into the shadows.

"And, till she come, as truly as to heaven I do confess the vices of my blood, So justly to your grave ears I'll present How I did thrive in this fair lady's love, And she in mine."

"Say it, Othello."

"Her father loved me," he said. "Often invited me to his house and company; ever eager to question me on the story of my life. From year to year he would press me—of battles fought, of sieges endured, and the fickle fortunes I had passed through."

He paused, his eyes dark with recollection.

"I ran it through," he continued, "from my earliest boyish days, up to the very hour he bade me speak. I spoke of disastrous chances, of moving accidents by flood and field, of hair-breadth escapes in the imminent deadly breach. Of being taken prisoner by the insolent foe, and sold into slavery; and how I was redeemed from thence. I told him of my bearing—my portance—in the chronicles of my travels."

A hush fell over those who listened, for even in that moment, the gravity of Othello's words pulled the room tight with attention.

"I told of antres vast and deserts idle, of rough quarries, rocks, and hills whose heads touch heaven. That was my cue to speak," he said, voice low and reverent. "Such was the process. I told of the Cannibals that eat each other—the Anthropophagi—and of men whose heads do grow beneath their shoulders."

He allowed the strangeness of it to settle, then added, "This to hear would Desdemona seriously incline. But the business of the household would oft draw her away. Yet, as soon as she could with haste dispatch her duties, she would return again—and with a greedy ear devour up my discourse." He smiled, almost shyly, at the memory.

"One evening, in a rare and quiet hour, when the clamour of the world seemed to pause in deference to the hush of fate, Desdemona, with a countenance serene but eyes alight with ardour, did entreat me—gently, yet with a fervour that belied her measured tone—to unfold the entirety of my tale. Not the half-formed echoes she had chanced to catch in corridors or parlours, but the whole chronicle. And so, with a heart both burdened and unburdened in the telling, I spoke." Othello sighed, almost as though he could hardly believe his own tale, he was reliving the moment his entire life had led towards, the moment where his past became his future. He let the silence spread like ink in water.

"I spoke of my youth, marred by misfortune and etched with the scars of peril; of escapes so narrow that even now I scarce believe them; of chains once clasped upon my limbs and the bitter taste of slavery undone. And as these words took flight, I beheld her countenance change—her eyes, wide and bright, did well with tears. She sat, statue-still, drinking in each syllable as though it were the very air, until, at length, my tale was told. Then, softly, with a breath that might have stirred the very stars, she gave me a world of sighs. "'Tis strange," she murmured, "passing strange. Pitiful. Wondrous pitiful." She declared that she wished she had not heard it, and yet—ah!—she wished also that Heaven had fashioned her such a man as I." Othello let out a low chuckle, as though it was he who were under a spell, not Desdemona. "With a gratitude most gracious, she thanked me. And then, with a subtlety that could shame the most seasoned courtier, she confessed—if aught could woo her, it would be a story such as mine." Othello cast eyes around the room. In that moment, the soldier was gone, and there stood for a moment a naïve man who had found love for the first and only time in his life.

The chamber held its breath. Othello paused, and with the solemn grace of one accustomed to ceremony but unaccustomed to laying bare his soul, drew a fine handkerchief from within the breast of his tunic. He pressed it once to the corner of his eye, no more than a gesture. It seemed as though he did it not to conceal emotion, but to acknowledge it, and to display his own self-mastery. The cloth bore a faint pattern of strawberries, almost faded now with time and touch. He folded it with a soldier's neatness, placing the red fruit in the bottom right corner as if obeying some private code, and returned it to its place with the practiced familiarity of something long kept and seldom explained. Then, gathering the silence like a cloak, he resumed his tale.

"Upon this hint, I spoke. She loved me for the dangers I had passed. And I loved her that she did pity them."

He straightened, noble in his declaration.

"This only is the witchcraft I have used," he said. And as if summoned by the very truth of that confession, Desdemona entered.

"Here comes the lady," said Othello. "Let her bear witness."

A murmuration of stillness passed through the chamber as Othello concluded his tale. It was the sort of silence that resists interruption, as though the very walls were reluctant to return to the mundane business of war and governance after such a revelation of the heart. The Doge, whose life had been spent among scrolls and statutes, leaned forward, touched, perhaps for the first time in many years, by the strange, clean gravity of unadorned truth.

"I think this tale would win my daughter too." He spoke quietly, but loud enough for the senators to hear, all of whom replied with a good-natured murmur of approving humour. It was no idle jest, but a deep compliment, a thread of olive branch spun through the needle-eye of statecraft. He turned to Brabantio, whose face, carved in fatherly anguish, had not softened, though his shoulders betrayed the slow loosening of a man who knows he has lost.

"Good Brabantio," said the Doge gently, "take this mangled matter as best you may. Men use their broken blades still — better that than fight with empty hands."

But the old patrician would not be soothed. "Let her speak," he said, fixing his daughter with the stare of a man daring to be proven wrong. "If she confesses she was half the wooer, then let destruction fall on my head, and none upon the man." He drew a sharp breath. "Come here, gentle mistress. In this hall of lords and law, where lies your deepest duty?"

All eyes turned to Desdemona.

She stepped forward — a pale shape in dove-grey silk, her movements solemn but unafraid. Though she looked a creature of tapestries and sonnets, her voice, when it came, was clear and true.

"My noble father," she began, "I do perceive here a divided duty."

The men in the chamber, many of them fathers themselves, shifted slightly. It was not a rebuke, but an unveiling — a daughter's love made articulate in terms they could understand, even admire.

"To you I am bound for life and education," she said, "for both teach me to honour and respect you. You are the lord of duty. I am your daughter."

She paused. A softness touched her voice.

"But here stands my husband. And as my mother once preferred you above her father, so do I now profess my duty to the Moor, my lord."

It was gently said — but final. The council understood it. So did Brabantio.

He turned away, as though to look upon her would salt the wound. "God be wi' you. I have done."

A silence hung. Then, bitterness stirred his voice again. "I would rather adopt a child than sire one. Come here, Moor."

Othello stepped forward.

Brabantio's hands tightened once at his sides, then opened — not in blessing, but in resignation.

"I give you that which, had you not already stolen, I would keep from you with all my heart. But take her, for take her you have. And let me be glad that I have no other child, for her escape would teach me cruelty — I should hobble the next with chains. I have done, my lord."

He stepped back into shadow.

The Doge, unwilling to let so raw a moment linger, spoke with the cadence of closing.

"Let me speak now in your fashion," he said, "and lay down a sentence as a stone laid in water: steadying, yet sinking."

He stood. The years showed on him suddenly.

"When remedies are past," he said, "then griefs must be past too. We cannot weep into the cup of fortune and expect it not to spill anew. Let patience mock the injury. Let he who has been robbed learn to smile — for in that smile, something is stolen back from the thief."

The words were wise. Yet Brabantio, for all his years, had no patience left.

"Let the Turk then take Cyprus," he said darkly, "and let us smile — for we are told that is the way to suffer nobly. Yet, my lords, the bruised heart is not healed through the ear. Words are not balm, but breath."

His voice dropped.

"I beg you — proceed to the affairs of state."

And so the Doge did.

He turned once more to Othello, the general whose very presence in this chamber now embodied both their highest hope and deepest controversy.

"The Turk," he said, "comes armed with all his strength — a most mighty preparation makes for Cyprus. And though Montano serves there capably, it is the common voice, the people's cry, that prefers you, Othello."

He raised a hand, his tone now brisk with necessity. "You must slubber the gloss of your new-found joy with the ironwork of war. We send you at once."

Othello bowed with grace unfeigned.

"Most grave senators," he said, "custom has long made war my bedding. I find, in hardship, not aversion but a kind of readiness. I accept this charge against the Ottomites with both humility and resolve."

But now his tone grew softer — not in doubt, but in gentleness.

"I must ask one thing. I entreat the Senate to see to a proper place for my wife — with the rank and comfort due to her breeding."

The Doge glanced to Brabantio. "Would you have her in your house, Signior?"

Brabantio's mouth tightened. "I will not have it so."

"Nor I," said Othello quickly.

Desdemona's voice rose like a lark above the low chorus of men.

"Nor I," she said, stepping forward again. "To remain in my father's house would stir his grief afresh. I would not be so unkind."

She turned to the Doge, her tone petitionary but assured.

"Most gracious Duke, let me unfold myself before your judgment, and find in your voice the licence I seek."

"What would you, Desdemona?"

"That I might go with my lord to Cyprus. I love him not only in name, but in presence. My heart is tuned to his. I saw not his skin, but his soul — and in that soul, his valour, his honour, his constancy."

The room was still.

"If he go to war," she said softly, "and I remain, then the very rites by which I love him are denied me. I would be a moth in peacetime, fluttering vainly in his absence. Let me go with him."

Othello reached for the echo.

"Let her have your voices," he said, turning to the Doge and the assembled senators. "This is not appetite that moves me. No lust, no heat, no indulgence of some withered fancy. If ever I let her presence interfere with the duties of my office, may my helm be used for kitchen pots and my name dragged through every indignity!"

He straightened, every inch the general now — and still, the man in love.

The Doge's voice carried the final note of authority across the flagstoned chamber.

"Let it be as you shall privately determine," he said, addressing Othello and Desdemona with a weary finality. "The affair cries haste, and haste must answer it."

"You must away to-night," added a senator, rising as the others did.

Othello nodded. "With all my heart."

"At nine in the morning, we reconvene," said the Doge. "Leave an officer behind to receive our commission — matters of import, instructions and provisions."

"So please your grace," said Othello, turning slightly, "my ancient shall remain. He is a man of honesty and trust. I place Desdemona's care in his hands."

Iago bowed, the image of deference. No man in that room would have guessed his blood ran black with envy.

"So be it," said the Duke. "Good night to all."

He turned one last time to Brabantio, whose face had grown stonier with each breath.

"And noble signior," said the Duke, "if virtue has beauty, then your son-in-law is fairer than black."

A clever balm, too little, too late. Brabantio stared, unblinking.

"Look to her, Moor," he said coldly, "if thou hast eyes to see. She has deceived her father — and may thee."

Iago heard the words but his face remained a mask. In his mind, however, pieces were moving, quietly, efficiently, across an invisible board. Brabantio departed without bow or farewell, the remnants of his pride trailing like torn silk behind him.

"My life upon her faith," he said, to Brabantio, to the room, to fate, to himself.

The chamber began to empty. Othello stood a moment longer, Desdemona beside him, her hand light upon his arm. Then he turned to Iago.

"Honest Iago, I leave Desdemona in your charge. Let your wife, Emilia, attend her. Bring them after me at the best advantage." And to Desdemona, in softer tone: "Come, love. We have but an hour to share — for love, for counsel, and for farewell. We must obey the time."

Their footsteps echoed off into the night.

...

As the last of the Senate shambled from the chamber, the torches dwindled to a weary flicker, casting long, uncertain shadows upon the marble floor. Only Roderigo lingered — a mooncalf of a man, all drooping shoulders and unspent tears, heartsick and heavy with despair. Iago remained as well, loitering under pretence of inspecting the chamber's architecture or some imagined flaw in the stonework, though in truth he watched Roderigo with the idle interest one might show a beetle tipped on its back.

"Iago," he said, voice thin,

Iago looked up from the patch of nothing he was pretending to occupy him.

"What say'st thou, noble heart?" he murmured, the words rounded with a tenderness that, for a moment, might have passed for genuine. There was something in his tone, enough to stir a blush in a lonely man.

"What shall I do now?"

"Why," replied Iago, smiling faintly, "go to bed, and sleep."

But Roderigo shook his head, wild-eyed. "I will incontinently drown myself."

Iago's eyebrows lifted with mock incredulity.

"If thou dost," he said briskly, "I shall never love thee after. Why, thou silly gentleman!"

"But it is silliness to live when to live is torment," Roderigo moaned. "We have a prescription when death is our physician."

"O Villainous!" Iago scoffed, drawing out the word with the laboured flourish of a street performer aping a dullard. "I have seen four times seven years, and in that time I have yet to meet a man who loved himself so little he'd drown over a woman. Drown? I would sooner trade places with a baboon than whimper thus for a guinea-hen."

"What should I do then?" Roderigo asked, pitiful as a dog whipped and returned. "I know it's shameful to be so fond — but it is not my virtue to amend it."

"Virtue?" Iago sneered. "A fig for virtue! It is in ourselves that we are thus," he puffed himself up, chest swelling like some regal amphibian. "or thus" he deflated at once, shoulders caving, breath spilling from him like wind from a bellows. "Our bodies are gardens to which our wills are gardeners." He began to pace, slowly, with the solemnity of a man delivering sacred wisdom, though his eyes gleamed with a light far more devilish than divine.

"So that if we will plant nettles or sow lettuce," he said, "set purifying hyssop and weed up thyme; supply it with one gender of herbs or distract it with many; either to have it sterile with idleness or manured with industry, why—" He paused, raising a finger as though pronouncing judgement upon the very laws of nature, "the power and corrigible authority of this lies in our wills."

He stopped, turned, and looked upon Roderigo with a mixture of disdain and pity, like a tutor addressing an unusually dense pupil. "If the balance of our lives had not one scale of reason to poise another of sensuality, the blood and baseness of our natures would conduct us to most preposterous conclusions."

He leaned in, voice softening into something more intimate, almost tender. "But we have reason, my friend, to cool our raging motions — our carnal stings, our unbitted lusts." He was very close to Roderigo now, hips almost touching.

And then, with the faintest tilt of his head, as though plucking the fruit of thought just as it ripened: "Whereof I take this that you call love to be a sect... or scion."

"It cannot be" mumbled Roderigo, though he was already feeling better.

Iago moved even closer now, pleased with his little horticultural conceit. The notion that love, in all its trembling finery, was merely a scion of lust's older rootstock, a sprig of vice dressed up as virtue, was probably the closest thing he had ever got to honesty. He moved his mouth close to Roderigo's ear, his tone low and rich with persuasion.

"It is merely a lust of the blood," Iago said, softly now, as if confiding some holy secret, "and a permission of the will."

He smiled, then suddenly scoffed, loud and scornful. "Come, be a man. Drown thyself? Drown cats and blind puppies, not men of wit and fortune! I have professed myself thy friend, Roderigo, and I confess me knit to thy deserving with cables of perdurable toughness."

His voice had become strangely coaxing, almost intimate.

"I could never better stead thee than now. Put money in thy purse."

He began to pace again, hands clasped behind his back, a schoolmaster again, but now with a more favourable student.

"Follow thou the wars; spoil that sweet face with a borrowed beard"—his hand traced Roderigo's baby-smooth cheeks—"I say again: put money in thy purse. It cannot be that Desdemona should long continue her love to the Moor—put money in thy purse—nor he his to her. It was a violent commencement, and thou shalt see an answerable sequestration. Put but money in thy purse." The smile now crooked with promise. "These Moors are changeable in their wills. Fill thy purse with money."

He paused, plucking a metaphor like ripe fruit from the air.

"The food that to him now is as luscious as locusts shall shortly be to him as bitter as coloquintida." He savoured the word — coloquintida — a thing bitter enough to curdle even a man's marrow. His eyes flashed.

"She must change for youth. When she is sated with his body, she will see the error of her choice. She must have change. She must. Therefore: put money in thy purse." He stepped back, spreading his hands in mock sanctimony. "If thou must needs damn thyself, do it in a more delicate way than drowning. Make all the money thou canst."

He drew a sharp breath and spat the rest like venom.

"If the holy pretence and paper-thin vow between that misled Moor and that supersubtle Venetian dame are not too hard for my wits and all the tribe of hell, then thou shalt enjoy her." Here, he stared into Roderigo's face, like a glaring contest. There was something of the clown in him now — a dark jester, puffed with his own cleverness, daring the world to call his bluff.

"A pox on drowning thyself! It is clean out of the way."

"And if she doesn't?" Roderigo muttered.

Iago spoke now with a dreadful intimacy, he looked older, Mephistophelean almost. The last of the nearby candles gave a final tremble and died, leaving the room bathed only in the moon's cold light. "Then you will at least have gained coin and experience. It is better to be hanged in the compassing of your joy than to drown having tasted nothing. You'd do well to wear the noose with a smile — if your lips still remember her kiss, however reluctant." He drew back, the smile lingering like smoke. "You understand me." He touched two fingers to Roderigo's sleeve with the intimacy of someone who had once untied many a purse by that same touch.

Roderigo nodded slowly. "You'll stand by me? If I depend upon the outcome?"

"Thou art sure of me," Iago said easily, clasping his arm. "Go, make money:--I have told thee often, and I re-tell thee again and again, I hate the Moor. We both have our reasons. Let's be joined in purpose. If you can make the Moor a cuckold, thou dost thyself a pleasure, me a sport. There are many events in the womb of time which will be delivered. Traverse! go, provide thy money. We will have more of this to-morrow. Adieu."

"And where shall I meet you?"

"At my lodging."

"I'll come early."

"Go to then. Farewell."

Roderigo began to leave, and Iago called after.

"One thing, Roderigo."

"What say you?"

"No more talk of drowning. Do you hear?"

"I am changed," Roderigo said, and with a kind of mad, pathetic energy, "I'll sell all my land."

Iago stood alone. The torchlight guttered in the wall sconces, shadows casting his face half in gold, half in gloom.

"Thus do I ever make my fool my purse," he said quietly. "If I spent time on such a snipe for anything but my gain, I would profane knowledge itself." A darker note entered his voice now — no longer cynical amusement, but something colder, more calculated.

"I hate the Moor." These words were spoken with such acidity that for a brief moment, Iago's entire face transformed into a mask of pure hatred. A livid vein stood out on his neck, and his breath became ragged. The moment passed after an instant, and he continued, muttering to himself like a man bewitched.

"And it is thought abroad, that 'twixt my sheets, he has done my office: I know not if 't be true, but I, for mere suspicion in that kind, will do as if for surety."

He holds me well; The better shall my purpose work on him. Cassio's a proper man: let me see now: To get his place and to plume up my will in double knavery. Let's see:--After some time, to abuse Othello's ear That Cassio is too familiar with his wife. Handsome, a smooth dispose, well-mannered. A face made to breed suspicion in jealous men. I will make Othello see in him what he fears most. To be suspected, framed to make women false. The Moor is of a free and open nature, That thinks men honest that but seem to be so. Othello will be as led as tenderly by the nose as asses are." He paused his malicious soliloquy, tilting his head as if he had heard some noise from within the shadows.

"I have it. It is engendered. Hell and night must bring this monstrous birth to the world's light."

He stepped forward, into the night, and melted into the shadows.

ACT II

The Island and the Mask

*In which Cyprus receives its players, reputations begin to curdle,
and the wind brings poison on its breath.*

ACT II SCENE 1

The harbour at Famagusta lay crouched beneath the lash of a storm that had galloped in from the Levant with all the fury of a scorned god. Waves struck the breakwaters like battering rams, each impact scattering a mist that hissed as it struck the lime-stained stone. The sky, grey as a debtor's sleeve and stitched with bruise-coloured clouds, bore down upon the Cypriot shore, while gulls screamed curses from their spinning orbits above. The island itself—a Venetian jewel clutched tight against the rising menace of Ottoman hands—seemed to shiver in its chains.

Montano, the governor deposed by appointment but not yet removed in soul, stood at the edge of the quay wrapped in a cloak of coarse wool, already soaked through and stained with salt. His eyes, seasoned by war and wind, peered into the indistinct blur of sea and sky.

"What from the cape can you discern at sea?" he asked the younger gentleman beside him—a lad with windburned cheeks and a moustache still learning its full ambition.

"Nothing at all," the young man replied, his voice raised above the gale, "'tis a highwrought flood. I cannot, 'twixt the heaven and the main, descry a sail."

The sea, indeed, had ceased to be sea and become some monstrous, grey-blue organ convulsing under the hand of God. Even ships hewn from the oak of Dalmatian forests and braced with Venetian steel were but driftwood in this madness.

Montano nodded grimly, squinting into the tumult. "The wind hath spoken loudly on land. A fuller blast ne'er shook our battlements. If it hath ruffian'd so upon the sea—what ribs of oak, when mountains melt upon them, can hold the mortise?"

A second gentleman joined them, face pinched and knuckles white from gripping the parapet of the outer fortress. "A segregation of the Turkish fleet," he reported, teeth chattering, "can be seen, or guessed at, from the northern cliff. The sea hath turned preacher—it casts up waves like accusations against the clouds. I never did see such molestation upon the enchafed flood."

The words, though poetic in their desperation, were not merely decorative. They painted the truth: if the Turkish fleet had not been shattered, it had been scattered.

"And if not embay'd," Montano muttered, "they are drowned."

Then came the cry—half-drowned in wind but sharp enough to turn every head. "News, lads! Our wars are done!"

The third gentleman—one of those indefatigable news-bringers who always seemed to have one foot in rumour and the other in blessed truth—bounded across the quay. His eyes were wide with the thrill of survival, and he bore the look of a man who had stared into Neptune's gullet and emerged with all limbs intact.

"The tempest hath so bang'd the Turks that their designment halts. A noble ship of Venice—a Veronesa, I think—hath seen the wreckage herself. Near total loss. The sea fought on our behalf."

Montano took this not with exultation, but with the sober nod of a man who knew how war ended—with salt in the lungs and mothers in black.

"But the Veronesa?" he asked.

"She is here," the man replied, breathlessly. "Michael Cassio's aboard. Lieutenant to the warlike Moor."

The mention of Othello's name lent the storm a pause, as though the wind itself held its breath.

Montano allowed himself the hint of a smile. "A worthy governor. I have served him—and the man commands like a full soldier."

He turned toward the brume-choked sea. "Let's to the seaside, ho! As well to see the vessel that's come in as to throw out our eyes for brave Othello—even till we make the main and the aerial blue an indistinct regard."

"Come, let's do so," said the third, already striding toward the quay. "For every minute is expectancy of more arrivance."

However, their progress was quickly checked by the appearance of a windswept Cassio, whose arrival, however, proved less triumphant than expected. He stepped ashore with the elegance of a courtier and the eyes of a sleepless soldier. The salt in his hair was not just from the sea—it was born of worry, which clung to him like a scent. His uniform bore no injury, but his face did.

"Gentlemen of Cyprus," he called, shaking wet hands with his new hosts, "I thank you, valiant hearts. Yet I am poor company today, for I have lost the Moor upon a dangerous sea."

Montano clasped his forearm with familiarity. "Is he well shipped?"

"Aye," Cassio nodded, "his bark is stoutly timbered, his pilot of very expert and approved allowance. Therefore my hopes—though they suffer not little—yet stand in bold cure."

But even as he spoke, a cry rose from the watchtowers above the dock: "A sail, a sail, a sail!"

They turned as one.

A fourth gentleman came running, hat clutched to his head, water streaming from his cloak. "Another ship—bearing north! She rides low, but she rides!" he shouted.

Cassio stepped forward, his heart already trying to leap from his chest.

"Let it be the Moor," he breathed. "Let it be him. What noise?"

The men surged towards the harbour's lip, the storm suddenly no more than the background music to this new, fragile hope. The sea may have bellowed like a wounded god, but all ears strained for the voice of Othello—or the sound of wood splintering against rock.

The storm, though softening, still grumbled like a hungover god above the town of Famagusta. The sky remained pewter-hued, shot through with uneasy veins of blue that flickered like remorse in the eyes of a liar. Rain no longer fell, but the clouds kept their arms folded as if to say: We are not finished yet.

Atop the sea-wall, the watchers had grown in number. Men, women, and children gathered in loose knots across the brow of the sea, straining their necks as though the very act of expectation might hasten the arrival. And then, a ripple through the crowd—a boy's voice shrieking, "A sail!"—and the cry took hold like wildfire on dry thatch.

Cassio heard it with his soul before he heard it with his ears. "My hopes do shape him for the governor," he murmured, hardly aware he'd spoken aloud. And then: boom—a low thunder not from the sky, but from the shore. Cannon-fire, but ceremonial, the ancient clatter of friendship in iron tongue.

"They do discharge their shot of courtesy," said the second gentleman beside him. "Our friends, at least."

Cassio nodded. "I pray you, sir, go forth, and give us truth who 'tis that is arrived."

The man bowed and dashed off through the mire.

Montano—always a man to steer conversation into deeper waters— glanced sideways. "But, good lieutenant… is your general wived?"

Cassio smiled—thinly at first, but then with a rising warmth, like wine kindled by a hearth. "Most fortunately. He hath achieved a maid that paragons description and wild fame. One that excels the quirks of blazoning pens, and in the essential vesture of creation does tire the ingener."

Such praise might have sounded rehearsed in another's mouth, but Cassio, with his courtly manners and open face, spoke of Desdemona with the reverence of a votary and the admiration of a man still too young to lie expertly. She was not merely beautiful—she was just and good, and in his soldier's mind, that made her terrifyingly rare.

Before Montano could reply, the second gentleman reappeared, panting slightly from his errand.

"Well?" asked Cassio.

"'Tis one Iago," the man reported, brushing rain from his sleeves. "Ancient to the general."

Cassio's brow lifted in pleased surprise. "Has had most favourable and happy speed. Tempests themselves, high seas and howling winds, the guttered rocks and congregated sands— those traitors waiting to trap an innocent keel—seemed, as if moved by beauty itself, to forget their natures and let the divine Desdemona pass unharmed."

Montano, perhaps more intrigued by the lady than the metaphysics, asked simply, "What is she?"

Cassio turned to him. "She that I spake of—our great captain's captain. Left in the conduct of the bold Iago, whose arrival here has outpaced all expectation by a full week. Great Jove, guard Othello and swell his sails with your own divine breath, that he may reach this bay safely in his tall ship, find his swift joy in Desdemona's arms, rekindle the fire in our weary hearts, and bring comfort to all Cyprus."

As though summoned by his very invocation, the approaching figures emerged from the quay's curve, half-veiled in storm-mist: a small entourage with wet cloaks, chattering servants, and four central players moving in half-military, half-aristocratic formality. At their head, radiant as the first star in a clearing sky, came Desdemona. Close at her side walked a dark-cloaked woman—her pace practical, her face unreadable—Emilia, wife to Iago. And just behind, with the stride of one rehearsing virtue and calculating opportunity, came Iago himself, flanked by the ever-hungering Roderigo, looking rather more goat than gallant.

Cassio's breath caught. "O, behold—the riches of the ship is come on shore!"

And then, bowing deeply—perhaps too deeply—he addressed the lady whose beauty so recently occupied his eloquence.

"Ye men of Cyprus," he called to those nearby, "let her have your knees. Hail to thee, lady! And the grace of heaven, before, behind thee, and on every hand, enclose you with divine protection!"

Desdemona returned the gesture with grace but also urgency, stepping forward through the crush of greetings. "I thank you, valiant Cassio. What tidings can you tell me of my lord?"

Cassio—always honest, even in disappointment—shook his head. "He is not yet arrived. Nor know I aught but that he's well, and will be shortly here."

Desdemona paled. "O, but I fear—how lost you company?"

He explained with a kind of weary poetry, "The great contention of the sea and skies parted our fellowship."

But before her fears could fully form, another cry from above: "A sail! A sail!" More cannon, echoing through the half-wrecked gullies like a chorus of heralds.

"They give their greeting to the citadel," noted the second gentleman. "This likewise is a friend."

Cassio turned to one of the guards. "See for the news."

Then, finally, as if just realising the others now stood beside them: "Good ancient, you are welcome."

He extended his courtly manners toward the two women. "Welcome, mistress." And to Emilia—whose eyes, already sharp with suspicion—he bowed and said with gentle formality, "Let it not gall your patience, good Iago, that I extend my manners; 'tis my breeding that gives me this bold show of courtesy."

With that, he took Emilia's hand, bowed over it, and placed a kiss upon her knuckles—light, polite, and entirely without guile.

But Iago, never one to let warmth pass unmocked, smirked like a serpent beneath a doublet.

"Sir," Iago said, his voice lacquered in ridicule, "if she gave you as much of her lips as she gives me of her tongue, you'd have more than your fill."

Desdemona, surprised by the jab, turned protectively to Emilia. "Alas—she has no speech!"

Iago gave a low chuckle. "In faith, too much. I find it still, when I try to sleep. Marry, before your ladyship, I'll grant—she keeps her tongue mostly in her heart and scolds me silently, in thought."

Emilia snapped, "You've little cause to say so."

But Iago was already rolling on, waving her off like a bothersome thought. "Come on, come on—you're portraits in public, bells in your parlours, wild-cats in your kitchens, saints when you suffer, devils when you're crossed, actresses in your housework, and housewives only in your beds."

A gasp rippled through the gathering—more shock than anger, as Iago's words seemed at once too scandalous for polite company and too familiar to be ignored.

"O fie upon thee, slanderer!" Desdemona exclaimed, but with half a smile, for the rain had softened tempers as much as it had sleeves.

"Nay, it is true," Iago insisted, "or else I am a Turk. You rise to play, and go to bed to work."

"I pray you," Emilia muttered, her voice flat with warning, "you shall not write my praise."

"No," Iago replied, "let me not."

And for a moment, his smile faltered—just slightly—as if he'd heard something truer than he meant to say.

Desdemona, with her hair swept back by the wind like a banner of moonlight, turned from the ramparts and fixed her eyes on Iago, who—though sodden—seemed none the less barbed for it.

"What wouldst thou write of me," she asked with a teasing solemnity, "if thou shouldst praise me?"

Iago gave a theatrical wince. "O gentle lady, do not put me to't; for I am nothing, if not critical."

"Come now, give it a try," she urged, stepping lightly over a puddle. "Has someone gone to harbour?"

"Ay, madam," he nodded, brushing the wet from his sleeves like dandruff from a philosopher's cloak.

She gazed down the coast, then lowered her eyes. "I am not merry," she confessed softly, "but I do beguile the thing I am by seeming otherwise." A half smile flickered on her lips, a candle behind cloudy glass. "Come, how wouldst thou praise me?"

Iago clasped his hands behind his back and tilted his head, as though searching the clouds for poetry. "I am about it," he said, "but indeed my invention comes from my pate as birdlime from rough cloth—it plucks out brains and all. But my Muse labours—and thus she is delivered in birth."

He cleared his throat with mock grandeur.

"If she's fair and wise," Iago declared, "then beauty and brains—well, one's for use, and the other knows how to use it."

Desdemona laughed. "Well said! And what if she's dark and clever?"

"If she's dark and clever," Iago shot back, "she'll find a fair man who likes her shade just fine."

"Worse and worse," Desdemona groaned.

Emilia snorted. "What if she's pretty and stupid?"

"She's never stupid, if she's pretty," said Iago, revelling in his own vulgar wisdom. "Even her foolishness finds her a husband."

Desdemona rolled her eyes. "These are old, ridiculous paradoxes to make drunkards laugh in taverns. What miserable praise have you for a woman who's both ugly and foolish?"

"There's none so ugly and foolish," Iago replied with a smirk, "who doesn't do the same dirty tricks the fair and clever ones do."

Desdemona gasped in mock offence. "O heavy ignorance! You praise the worst women best. But what praise could you possibly give to a truly deserving woman—one so good that even malice would have to vouch for her?"

Now Iago straightened, and for the briefest moment, there was a flicker of something sincere—perhaps admiration, perhaps disdain— hard to say. But the rhyme began to flow like a sermon with a smile.

"She who was fair and never proud,
Spoke when she chose, but never loud;
Had gold to spend, but never flaunted,
Resisted what she dearly wanted—"
He began to pace, the rhythm winding tighter.

"She who, though wronged and quick to strike,
Held back her wrath and spared the like;
Was never foolish in her reason,
And knew a cod's head from a salmon's in season;
Could think, yet never speak her mind,
And watched her suitors, but stayed behind—
She was a woman, if ever one walked the earth—"
Desdemona raised an eyebrow. "To do what?"

Iago grinned, wicked as a tavern door swinging open: "To nurse fools and write down the price of cheap ale."

A mix of gasps, chuckles, and groans broke through the group. Emilia's glare could have withered ivy.

Desdemona shook her head. "O most lame and impotent conclusion! Learn nothing from him, Emilia, though he be your husband."

She turned to Cassio. "What say you? Is he not a most profane and extravagant counsellor?"

Cassio gave an apologetic shrug. "He speaks home, madam. You may relish him more in the soldier than in the scholar."

But Iago was no longer listening to them. He watched as Cassio bowed toward Desdemona again, his fingers brushing hers in a courtly flourish.

He watched them closely—Cassio taking her hand, whispering soft as steam from a wine cup. Yes, Iago thought, just so. With a web no thicker than this—a palm pressed here, a smile offered there—he would trap as grand a fly as Cassio. Let him grin, let him flatter. He would be shackled by his own courtship soon enough.

He watched, hawk-like.

Yes… you say true. That's it exactly. If gestures like these—graceful, gallant, just rehearsed enough—could cost Cassio his commission, then perhaps he'd have done better never to have kissed his fingers so often.

Cassio did it again.

There it was—those three fingers to the lips, like a nobleman of Verona or a boy at court playing at courtesy. Very good. Well kissed! An excellent flourish.

And again.

Iago's lip curled. Would they were clyster-pipes for your sake, he thought. You'd be better served with a purge than another pantomime of grace. Those old enema tubes the physicians used to purge the body of its filth. Cassio needed one—for the soul, if not the stomach.

A trumpet blew from the harbour gates—brazen and bold, a sovereign sound.

Iago stiffened. "The Moor. I know his trumpet."

71

Cassio's face lit up. "'Tis truly so."

Desdemona turned toward the path that wound along the quay. "Let's meet him, and receive him."

"Lo, where he comes!" cried Cassio, and they all turned as a column of soldiers emerged from the mist.

At their head strode Othello.

He looked every inch the conqueror—broad-chested, eyes aflame with joy, cloak clinging damp to his shoulders, the silver-threaded hilt of his sword gleaming at his hip. And yet it was his face—his unguarded, thunderstruck expression—that made the air hush.

"O my fair warrior!" he cried.

"My dear Othello!" Desdemona flew to him, laughter and relief mingled in her voice like sunlight catching dew.

"It gives me wonder great as my content," said Othello, gathering her into his arms, "to see you here before me. O my soul's joy! If after every tempest come such calms, may the winds blow till they have waken'd death! Let the labouring bark climb hills of seas Olympus-high, and duck again as low as hell's from heaven!"

He drew back slightly, gazing at her as though her presence restructured the logic of thought.

"If I were now to die," he said, voice low and shaken, "'twere now to be most happy. For I fear my soul hath her content so absolute, that not another comfort like to this succeeds in unknown fate."

"The heavens forbid," Desdemona said, touching his cheek, "but that our loves and comforts should increase, even as our days do grow."

"Amen to that, sweet powers," said Othello. "I cannot speak enough of this content. It stops me here; it is too much of joy—"

He kissed her. Long and public and without shame.

"—and this," he said softly, "and this, the greatest discords be."

And as he kissed her again, the drums of Cyprus beat faintly in the distance—echoes of a different storm, not of nature, but of men and jealousy and fate, already stirring beneath the surface of this newfound calm, yet the air around Othello and Desdemona, still echoing with their embraces, had the fragrant stillness of a battlefield just conquered. The wind had gentled, the clouds turned passive. A few soft drops fell like tears upon the bay, but the heavens seemed loath to interrupt what love had momentarily restored.

As Othello held her close—his mighty arms wrapped like battlements about her delicate form—he whispered, "That e'er our hearts shall make!" and kissed her once again. A sigh passed through the gathered crowd, half out of admiration, half out of envy.

But not all eyes were kind.

Iago stood a little apart. Rainwater dripped from his nose like slow ink from a pen. He watched them with the look of a man staring into a mirror and seeing not himself but the man he wished undone.

Oh, they're well-tuned now, he thought, watching the couple. Sweet music, for the moment. But I'll loosen the pegs that keep it in harmony soon enough—as honest as I am.

His grin twisted slightly, as if the lie tasted especially fine in the mouth.

Othello, meanwhile, turned to the assembled Cypriots with a great and generous warmth, his voice now bearing the rich timbre of command.

"Come, let us to the castle. News, friends: our wars are done. The Turks are drown'd."

There was a smattering of applause—some real, some ritual—and murmurs of thanksgiving to saints and sea alike.

Othello clasped Montano's hand, then nodded to the others. "How does my old acquaintance of this isle?" he asked, but barely waited for the answer before turning once more to Desdemona.

"Honey," he said softly, "you shall be well desired in Cyprus. I have found great love amongst them."

And he had. The men who saw him saw their protector. The women who saw her saw beauty, yes—but also serenity, grace, and a promise of goodness, rare as rain in a soldier's soul.

"O my sweet," he continued, now stumbling over the excess of his own affection, "I prattle out of fashion, and I dote in mine own comforts."

It was the closest thing to embarrassment he had ever worn in public—a proud general turned bashful groom, a lion made mild by the touch of a dove.

He cleared his throat, and with a sudden return to form, addressed his ancient.

"I prithee, good Iago, go to the bay and disembark my coffers. Bring thou the master to the citadel. He is a good one, and his worthiness does challenge much respect."

He laid a brief hand on Iago's shoulder—just long enough to speak trust, just short enough not to notice the shoulder stiffen beneath it.

"Come, Desdemona," he said, and the lovers turned from the dock, hands entwined.

"Once more," Othello added, with a smile full of heat and hope, "well met at Cyprus."

The crowd followed them with their eyes as they disappeared up the sloping causeway toward the fortified heart of the island. Soldiers began to disperse, townsfolk retreated to their windows, and the sea resumed its slow, breathy rasp against the shore.

Only Iago lingered.

He stood alone on the quay, the wind now curling about him like a petulant child tugging at a coat hem. His face had returned to neutrality, that dangerous middle ground between smile and scowl where his truest thoughts festered.

A boy passed him—a cabin-page from the Veronesa—humming a tune he'd likely picked up in the taverns of Venice. Iago stopped him with a look.

"What music's that?" he asked.

The boy shrugged. "A love song, sir."

Iago nodded. "Aye. A love song."

And as he turned toward the bay, where the last of the ships bobbed and strained at anchor, he muttered low to himself, "Then let me see the tuning undone. Let me break the strings—one by one—and silence this music, sweet as it may seem. For honest I am…"

And with that, he walked off toward the wharf, where Othello's coffers waited—unaware that inside them travelled not only silks and letters, but the seeds of ruin.

...

The sun was long vanished, though its ghost remained smeared in streaks of red and purple along the western edge of Cyprus. Torches guttered in iron sconces along the causeway to the citadel. The sea, grown quieter now, sighed like a great beast falling asleep.

Iago turned to Roderigo, who trailed him with a faithful dog's gaze—hungry, trusting, and just dim enough to be useful.

"Do thou meet me presently at the harbour," he said in a low, confidential tone. Then, drawing the young fool a little aside beneath a tangle of fig vines heavy with dusk's perfume, he gestured sharply. "Come hither. If thou be'st valiant—as they say base men being in love have then a nobility in their natures more than is native to them—list me."

He did not wait for assent.

"The lieutenant tonight watches on the court of guard. First—I must tell thee this—Desdemona is directly in love with him."

Roderigo blinked. "With him? Why, 'tis not possible."

Iago smiled, a curving, shadowed thing. "Lay thy finger thus." He pressed a gloved fingertip to his own temple. "And let thy soul be instructed."

He circled slowly, as if lecturing in some demonic schoolroom.

"Mark me with what violence she first loved the Moor—but for bragging and telling her fantastical lies. And will she love him still for prating? Let not thy discreet heart think it. Her eye must be fed."

He stepped closer, his words now slick with venom.

"And what delight shall she have to look on the devil? When the blood is made dull with the act of sport, there should be—again, to inflame it and give satiety a fresh appetite—loveliness in favour, sympathy in years, manners and beauties. All which the Moor is defective in."

A pause. Then softly, dangerously:

"Now, for want of these… her delicate tenderness will find itself abused, begin to heave the gorge, disrelish, and abhor the Moor. Very nature will instruct her in it and compel her to some second choice."

He threw open his arms in mock generosity. "Now, sir, this granted—as it is a most pregnant and unforced position—who stands so eminent in the degree of this fortune as Cassio does?"

He spat the name as though it burned.

"A knave very voluble; no further conscionable than in putting on the mere form of civil and humane seeming—for the better compassing of his salt and most hidden loose affection. Why, none—why, none!"

His voice rose with feverish conviction.

"A slipper and subtle knave. A finder of occasions. That has an eye can stamp and counterfeit advantages, though true advantage never present itself. A devilish knave!"

He let the echo ring out over the parapet.

"Besides," he added with bitter precision, "the knave is handsome, young, and hath all those requisites in him that folly and green minds look after. A pestilent complete knave. And the woman hath found him already."

Roderigo wrinkled his brow. "I cannot believe that in her; she's full of most blessed condition."

"Blessed fig's-end!" Iago snapped. "The wine she drinks is made of grapes! If she had been blessed, she would never have loved the Moor. Blessed pudding!"

He leaned in now, conspirator to conspirator.

"Didst thou not see her paddle with the palm of his hand?"

"I… yes, that I did," Roderigo admitted, "but that was but courtesy."

"Lechery, by this hand!" Iago hissed. "An index and obscure prologue to the history of lust and foul thoughts. They met so near with their lips, their breaths embraced together. Villainous thoughts, Roderigo! When these mutualities so marshal the way, hard at hand comes the main exercise—the incorporate conclusion, bodies adjoined in lust. Pish!"

He wheeled about, all mocking scorn and dangerous purpose.

"But sir, be you ruled by me. I have brought you from Venice. Watch you tonight. For the command—I'll lay't upon you. Cassio knows you not. I'll not be far from you. Do you find some occasion to anger him—speak too loud, taint his discipline, or what other course you please. The time shall more favourably minister."

Roderigo, eyes narrowing with hopeful malice, nodded. "Well."

Iago's voice grew sly, coaxing: "He is rash. Very sudden in choler. Haply may strike at you. Provoke him that he may—for even out of that will I cause these of Cyprus to mutiny. Whose qualification shall come into no true taste again but by the displanting of Cassio."

He took a slow, triumphant breath.

"So shall you have a shorter journey to your desires, by the means I shall then have to prefer them. And the impediment—most profitably removed—without which, there were no expectation of our prosperity."

Roderigo, a man with more beard than wit, grinned with ignorant complicity. "I will do this, if I can bring it to any opportunity."

Iago clapped him on the shoulder. "I warrant thee. Meet me by and by at the citadel. I must fetch his necessaries ashore. Farewell."

"Adieu," said Roderigo, departing like a pawn pushed two squares forward.

And now, at last, Iago stood alone, as he preferred it—Cyprus darkening around him, the warm air tinged with salt and sinister opportunity.

He paced, slow and deliberate, words no longer spoken to Roderigo but to the void, to the stars, to anyone—or no one—who dared overhear.

"That Cassio loves her, I do well believe it. That she loves him—it's apt and of great credit."

He paused.

"The Moor—howbeit that I endure him not—is of a constant, loving, noble nature. And I dare think he'll prove to Desdemona a most dear husband."

His tone darkened.

"Now—I do love her too."

He stopped.

"Not out of absolute lust—though given the chance I might stand accountant for as great a sin—but that's only a small ingredient that's led to diet my revenge."

He turned his gaze to the sea, dark and swaying like the mind he hid behind civility.

"For that I do suspect the lusty Moor hath leap'd into my seat." His mind reeled with the image of Othello and Emilia coiled together in coitus, and shuddered. "The thought whereof doth, like a poisonous mineral, gnaw my inwards. And nothing can or shall content my soul till I am even'd with him, wife for wife."

He took a long breath through his nose, as if savouring the scent of vengeance.

"Or failing so… yet that I put the Moor at least into a jealousy so strong that judgment cannot cure."

And then, with a flick of his fingers:

"If this poor fool from Venice—this trash I drag along like a hound on a scent—if he's willing to be used, then I'll have Michael Cassio exactly where I want him. I'll smear him to the Moor in the foulest fashion—for truth be told, I suspect Cassio may've worn my night-cap too."

A bitter laugh broke from his throat, as his wife took a procession of imaginary lovers, all wearing the faces of his social superiors. His blood boiled before evaporating, plasma fuelled his thoughts now.

"Make the Moor thank me, love me, and reward me… for making him egregiously an ass and practising upon his peace and quiet—even to madness."

He shook his head slowly, eyes alive with terrible delight.

"'Tis here," he said, "but yet confused. Knavery's plain face is never seen till used."

And with that, he turned toward the castle—his cloak sweeping the stones like a curtain falling at the end of an act—leaving only footsteps and fate in his wake.

ACT II SCENE 2

Evening crept down from the hills behind Famagusta like a velvet curtain, and with it, a sense of expectancy fell upon the town. The storm had scattered, the ships were docked, and the Mediterranean now mirrored the last flames of daylight with deceptive serenity. Torches began to sputter into life across the cobbled streets, their orange tongues licking at the dusk like celebrants preparing for a festival—or mourners cloaked in joy.

Down one of the central thoroughfares strode a figure in the livery of the citadel, a scarlet sash clapping at his hip with every purposeful step. Behind him trailed a small assembly—soldiers, merchants, children with almond-sweet breath and wide eyes—all drawn by the promise of spectacle. The man stopped beneath a mounted torch-bracket and raised a scroll.

"Hear all! Hear all!" cried the Herald, his voice cutting the street like a bugle-note.

The crowd leaned in. Housewives stilled their ladles; a wine-merchant pressed a cork back into its bottle.

"It is Othello's pleasure," the Herald declared, "our noble and valiant general, that, upon certain tidings now arrived—importing the mere perdition of the Turkish fleet—every man put himself into triumph."

A ripple of satisfaction moved through the people. The Turks—those distant, looming shadows—had been scattered by sea and storm. Fewer funerals. Fewer letters home written with blood.

"Some to dance," the Herald continued, "some to make bonfires—each man to what sport and revels his addiction leads him."

Here a boy cheered prematurely, and was hushed by a matron with a rolled apron.

"For, besides these beneficial news," the Herald went on, "it is the celebration of his nuptial."

Now that drew murmurs. Not all had yet seen the lady. Fewer still knew what to make of her.

"So much," he added, "was his pleasure should be proclaimed. All offices are open! And there is full liberty of feasting from this present hour of five—until the bell have told eleven."

The torch above him hissed, spitting sap.

"Heaven bless the isle of Cyprus," the Herald finished, "and our noble general, Othello!"

There came cheers at last, half sincere, half polite, like the echoes one offers to gods or governors. Then the crowd dispersed in a dozen directions—some to taverns, some to courtyards, some to fetch fiddles or fireworks, or to stoke old quarrels with new wine.

But the air, for all its festivity, was not altogether light. For though liberty had been declared, and Cyprus was spared the sabre this day, there lingered still a scent—intangible, yet metallic—of something not quite right. The sort of smell that clings to brass after it has been struck.

For the devil had not been drowned with the Turks.

He was still ashore.

ACT II SCENE 3

The hall was not grand. It bore the marks of military austerity barely dressed for festivity: a long table, roughly scrubbed, bore platters of spiced meats, roasted olives, and orange-peel piled like coals in little silver dishes. The floor was swept but stained, the sconces fresh-lit, and outside the tall windows, the lamps of Cyprus twinkled like drunken stars fallen into the harbour.

Othello entered with Desdemona on his arm, Cassio trailing behind like a man fresh from ceremony, already half-undone by the theatre of joy. The general wore a look of calm command, tempered by the gentle heat of love recently kindled. Desdemona, pale and incandescent, held her husband's arm with the ease of one who trusted in both the soldier and the man.

"Good Michael," said Othello, pausing near the great door, "look you to the guard tonight. Let's teach ourselves that honourable stop— not to outsport discretion."

There was no rebuke in it. Only a soldier's caution, fatherly and fond.

Cassio bowed. "Iago hath direction what to do," he said, "but notwithstanding, with my personal eye will I look to't."

Othello clapped him once on the shoulder. "Iago is most honest." The words were tossed off with the confidence of a man who sees the world clearly—and does not yet know that his lens has already been smeared with poison.

"Michael, good night. To-morrow with your earliest, let me have speech with you."

Then, with the softest glance toward his wife: "Come, my dear love. The purchase made, the fruits are to ensue. That profit's yet to come 'twixt me and you. Good night."

And they departed, leaving Cassio alone—though not for long.

Through the far door strolled Iago, bearing the look of a man who had just passed through the kitchen and taken stock of every wine-jug therein.

Cassio offered a nod. "Welcome, Iago; we must to the watch."

"Not this hour, lieutenant," said Iago, waving off the notion with a loose-fingered hand. "'Tis not yet ten o' the clock. Our general cast us thus early—for the love of his Desdemona; who, let us not therefore blame: he hath not yet made wanton the night with her, and she is sport for Jove."

Cassio, flushed and freshly earnest, replied, "She's a most exquisite lady."

"And, I'll warrant her," added Iago, "full of game."

"Indeed, she's a most fresh and delicate creature."

"What an eye she has," Iago murmured, stepping close. "Methinks it sounds a parley of provocation."

Cassio half-laughed, half-sighed. "An inviting eye... and yet methinks right modest."

"And when she speaks," said Iago, "is it not an alarum to love?"

Cassio gave it honestly. "She is indeed perfection."

"Well," said Iago, smirking now, "happiness to their sheets! Come, lieutenant, I have a stoup of wine—and here without are a brace of Cyprus gallants that would fain have a measure to the health of black Othello."

Cassio looked pained. "Not tonight, good Iago. I have very poor and unhappy brains for drinking. I could well wish courtesy would invent some other custom of entertainment."

"O, they are our friends," Iago cajoled. "But one cup! I'll drink for you."

Cassio gave a helpless gesture. "I have drunk but one cup tonight, and that was craftily qualified too. And behold what innovation it makes here." He tapped his temple. "I am unfortunate in the infirmity, and dare not task my weakness with any more."

"What, man!" Iago laughed. "'Tis a night of revels. The gallants desire it."

"Where are they?"

"Here at the door. I pray you, call them in."

Cassio, still shaking his head, moved to do so. "I'll do't—but it dislikes me."

As he exited, Iago leaned against a column and folded his arms.

If I can fasten but one cup upon him, he thought, with that which he hath drunk to-night already, he'll be as full of quarrel and offence as my young mistress' dog.

He grinned, remembering.

Now, my sick fool Roderigo—whom love hath turn'd almost the wrong side out—hath to-night caroused potations pottle-deep; pissed as a fart. And he's to watch. Three lads of Cyprus, noble swelling spirits, I've fluster'd with flowing cups. They watch too.

He paused, then murmured, "'Mongst this flock of drunkards am I to put our Cassio in some action that may offend the isle. But here they come…"

Cassio returned—now with Montano and a brace of cheerful rogues behind him. Servants followed with flagons, tankards, and a jug so wide-bellied it looked like it had swallowed a monk.

"'Fore God," said Cassio, "they have given me a rouse already."

"Good faith," Montano chuckled, "a little one—not past a pint, as I am a soldier."

"Some wine, ho!" cried Iago, snatching a tankard and launching into song:

"And let me the canakin clink, clink;
And let me the canakin clink—
A soldier's a man;
A life's but a span;

Why then, let a soldier drink!"

The room began to warm. Jokes stirred like smoke from candles. Plates clattered. Tankards clinked.

Cassio grinned. "'Fore God, an excellent song."

"I learned it in England," said Iago, raising his brow, "where, indeed, they are most potent in potting. Your Dane, your German, and your swag-bellied Hollander—drink, ho!—are nothing to your English."

"Is your Englishman so expert in his drinking?" asked Cassio, already refilling.

"Why, he drinks you," Iago nodded, "with facility—your Dane dead drunk. He sweats not to overthrow your Almain. He gives your Hollander a vomit ere the next pottle can be filled."

"To the health of our general!" cried Cassio, raising his mug.

Montano echoed, "I am for it, lieutenant—and I'll do you justice!"

Iago burst again into song, this time more comically than tunefully:

"King Stephen was a worthy peer,
His breeches cost him but a crown;
He held them sixpence all too dear,
With that he call'd the tailor lown—
He was a wight of high renown,
And thou art but of low degree—
'Tis pride that pulls the country down,
Then take thine auld cloak about thee!"

"Some wine, ho!" he shouted, slamming his mug down with theatrical gusto. And as the wine flowed, and Cassio laughed, and Montano clapped along to the rhythm of ruin, the Devil of Venice leaned in with the face of a friend.

It was, by the moon's estimation, no later than the tenth hour, and already the castle hall had lost all sense of rank or form. Cups had multiplied like mice, voices raised themselves into ladders, and every jest had found its echo, louder and less comprehensible than the last. The air swam with fumes—cinnamon, sour wine, old sweat, and spilled vinegar. Somewhere, a plate clattered to the floor and was not retrieved.

Cassio sat half-upright on a bench of dubious stability, blinking slowly at a flagon that seemed to regard him with equal suspicion.

"Why," he said, with the conviction of a man delivering his third truth of the evening, "this is a more exquisite song than the other."

Iago leaned over him, grinning like a man about to sell you a goat with three legs and a noble pedigree.

"Will you hear't again?"

"No." Cassio raised a finger—judicial, trembling. "For I hold him to be unworthy of his place that does those things."

"What things?"

Cassio stared, momentarily perplexed, then recovered.

"Well," he declared, "God's above all. And there be souls must be saved… and there be souls must not be saved."

Iago, with the smooth assurance of a priest catching a fly in a chalice, nodded. "It's true, good lieutenant."

"For mine own part," Cassio continued, weaving like a priest in a windstorm, "no offence to the general, nor any man of quality—I hope to be saved."

"And so do I too, lieutenant."

"Ay," said Cassio, pointing sternly at Iago, "but by your leave, not before me. The lieutenant is to be saved before the ancient. Let's have no more of this. Let's to our affairs. Forgive us our sins!"

He staggered to his feet, arms flung wide in theatrical absolution. "Gentlemen! Let's look to our business. Do not think, gentlemen, I am drunk." He jabbed at the air. "This is my ancient—this is my right hand, and this is my left." Cassio considered that hand a moment, trying to remember if he'd been wearing gloves or not. "I am not drunk now. I can stand well enough... and speak well enough."

All clapped and cheered—more for the effort than the outcome.

"Excellent well!" they cried.

Cassio nodded triumphantly, turned on his heel, and immediately exited into a wall he had not expected to be there.

Montano chuckled. "To the platform, masters. Come, let's set the watch."

But Iago lingered.

"You see this fellow that is gone before," he said, drawing Montano aside as the others filed out. "He is a soldier fit to stand by Caesar, and give direction. And do but see his vice."

He gestured to the stained floor, the reeling shadows, the long trail of broken dignity.

"'Tis to his virtue a just equinox—the one as long as the other. 'Tis pity of him."

Montano, frowning now, glanced toward the door.

Iago let the words hang, as if reluctant to say them. "I do fear the trust Othello puts in him," he said softly. "There may come a moment—some unfortunate lapse—when his weakness gets the better of him. And then... well. This island may feel the tremor."

"But is he often thus?" Montano asked.

"Evermore the prologue to his sleep," Iago said smoothly. "Timepieces would be well named after him, he spends twice as long in bed, if drink rock not his cradle."

Montano frowned deeper. "It were well the general were put in mind of it. Perhaps he sees it not. Or his good nature prizes the virtue that appears in Cassio, and looks not on his evils. Is that not true?"

But Iago had caught sight of a slinking figure—Roderigo, circling like a rat round a pie.

He used his eyes to instruct his pawn on the next move. Roderigo nodded and crept off like a man wearing too many secrets and not enough sense.

Montano remained in quiet consternation. "'Tis great pity that the noble Moor should hazard such a place as his own second with one of an ingraft infirmity. It were an honest action to say so to the Moor."

"Not I," said Iago, with mock protestation. "Not I, for this fair island. I do love Cassio well, and would do much—to cure him of this evil—"

A scream.

A crashing of furniture.

A bottle smashed.

"Help! Help!"

They turned—and Cassio re-entered, blood in his eye, dragging Roderigo behind him like a sack of curses.

"You rogue!" Cassio bellowed. "You rascal!"

Montano rushed forward. "What's the matter, lieutenant?"

"A knave teach me my duty? I'll beat the knave like a picnic basket!"

"Beat me?!" Roderigo squealed.

Cassio raised his arm—"Dost thou prate, rogue?"—and brought it down upon him. The blow landed with the satisfying slap of meat upon fate.

Montano lunged. "Nay, good lieutenant—hold your hand!"

But Cassio wrenched free. "Let me go, sir, or I'll knock you o'er the mazzard!"

Montano, ever the old soldier, shoved back. "Come, come—you're drunk!"

"Drunk?!"

The word detonated like gunpowder.

And then—the brawl began.

Chairs overturned. Tankards flew. One of the Cypriot gallants ducked beneath a table; another swung a ladle with the passion of a bishop at Mass. Cassio, blind with offence, struck at all comers, while Roderigo, nimble with terror, darted away toward the door like a spooked hare.

As Roderigo crawled away, baffled and bleeding, Iago whispered as he passed: "Away, I say—go out and cry mutiny!"

Roderigo fled, bellowing like a town-crier gone mad.

"Nay, good lieutenant!" Iago shouted, pressing into the fray with hypocritical hands. "Alas, gentlemen—help, ho! Lieutenant—sir—Montano—sir! Help, masters! Here's a goodly watch indeed!"

A bell rang. Loud and sudden.

Doom in brass.

"Who's that which rings the bell?" cried Iago. "Diablo, ho! The town will rise! God's will, lieutenant, hold! You will be shamed forever!"

Cassio, half-blind with fury, reeled back to strike again. Montano stepped forward to restrain him—and caught the blow instead.

Steel kissed flesh. Not a deep wound, but jagged, slicing through linen and skin as Montano twisted away. He staggered, clutching his side. Blood bloomed through his tunic.

And then— Othello was there.

The brawl had unspooled like a sailor's coil cast into the sea, fast and irretrievable, but Othello's entrance cut the rope clean. He came through the archway like judgement made flesh—shoulders broad with authority, his cloak still unfastened from bed, his eyes sharpened not by anger alone, but by the disappointment that is a soldier's deepest wound.

His voice, though level, carried through the hall like a clarion. "What is the matter here?"

Montano staggered forward, blood soaking the linen wound hastily pressed to his side. "'Zounds," he gasped, "I bleed still. I am hurt to the death—"

And down he went, folding like a broken standard, his limbs twitching once before stilling.

"Hold, for your lives!" Othello barked.

"Hold, ho!" echoed Iago, now suddenly all dutiful panic. "Lieutenant—sir—Montano—gentlemen—have you forgot all sense of place and duty? Hold! The general speaks to you—hold, hold, for shame!"

The bell tolled behind them, wild as a ship's warning clapper in fog. Othello raised a hand. "How now, ho! From whence ariseth this? Are we turned Turks, and to ourselves do that which heaven hath forbid the Ottomites?"

The accusation was not lightly made. To a Venetian officer, to be likened to a Turk was not merely slander—it was sacrilege.

"For Christian shame," he growled, "put by this barbarous brawl. He that stirs next to carve for his own rage holds his soul light—he dies upon his motion."

At once, silence dropped like a funeral shroud. The drunken, the foolish, the half-guilty—all froze.

"Silence that dreadful bell!" Othello commanded, eyes sweeping across the wounded, the watchers, the very stones of the place. "It frights the isle from her propriety. What is the matter, masters?"

His gaze fell on Iago. "Honest Iago," he said—how easily that word passed his lips, how cruelly it would return—"you that look'st dead with grieving, speak. Who began this? On thy love, I charge thee."

Iago bowed his head, his voice a tapestry of sorrow. "I do not know. Friends all but now, even now, in quarter and in terms like bride and groom devesting them for bed. And then—but now—as if some planet had unwitted men—swords out, and tilting one at other's breast, in opposition bloody. I cannot speak any beginning to this

95

peevish odds. And would in action glorious I had lost those legs that brought me to a part of it!"

Cassio, nearby, swaying, covered his face with a hand slick with sweat. Othello turned to him.

"How comes it, Michael, you are thus forgot?"

Cassio could only whisper, "I pray you, pardon me. I cannot speak."

Then Othello turned to Montano—who, though pale, struggled upright with the assistance of a page and a sergeant.

"Worthy Montano," said the general, "you were wont be civil. The gravity and stillness of your youth the world hath noted, and your name is great in mouths of wisest censure. What's the matter that you unlace your reputation thus, and spend your rich opinion for the name of a night-brawler? Give me answer to it."

Montano drew breath between his teeth. "Worthy Othello, I am hurt to danger. Your officer, Iago, can inform you— while I, for the moment, must spare my breath, as the effort offends me."

He winced as the wound was probed. "Nor know I aught by me that's said or done amiss this night… unless self-charity be sometimes a vice, and to defend ourselves it be a sin when violence assails us."

Now, Othello's calm was visibly cracked. His nostrils flared.

"Now, by heaven," he said, voice low and edged, "my blood begins my safer guides to rule; and passion, having my best judgement collied, assays to lead the way."

He raised a single hand—not high, but firm—and the hall seemed to shrink from it.

"If I once stir," he warned, "or do but lift this arm, the best of you shall sink in my rebuke. Give me to know how this foul rout began. Who set it on?"

His voice dropped a note, intimate and lethal.

"And he that is approved in this offence, though he had twinned with me—both at a birth—shall lose me."

There it was: the finality. Othello, ever generous, could not abide chaos among his ranks. Not here. Not now.

"What! In a town of war—yet wild—the people's hearts brimful of fear—to manage private and domestic quarrel? In night? And on the court and guard of safety? 'Tis monstrous. Iago—who began't?"

Montano, lips white, added quietly, "If partially affined, or leagued in office, thou dost deliver more or less than truth, thou art no soldier."

Iago raised his palms. "Touch me not so near. I had rather have this tongue cut from my mouth than it should do offence to Michael Cassio."

Iago cupped his mouth with his hands, as if he had spoken the name of some great secret by mistake. Then, as if reluctantly pulled toward duty by honour alone, he began to speak. He glanced at Cassio, his eyes filled with genuine-looking remorse. Cassio returned the look, sober now, resigned. Truth was part of the code, and Iago, honest Iago, could tell no lie. They all knew it.

Iago continued, "Yet I persuade myself, to speak the truth shall nothing wrong him. Thus it is, general."

He recounted the event with masterful neutrality—every word weighed, every omission deliberate. Roderigo became "a fellow crying out for help." Cassio became "determined." Montano "stepped in." Iago, the intervening angel, "pursued." And when he returned, there were swords again—"at blow and thrust."

"More of this matter cannot I report," he concluded. "But men are men. The best sometimes forget. Though Cassio did some little wrong to him—as men in rage strike those that wish them best—yet surely Cassio received from him that fled some strange indignity, which patience could not pass."

Othello was silent a moment. Then:

"I know, Iago, thy honesty and love doth mince this matter, making it light to Cassio."

He turned to his lieutenant. "Cassio, I love thee. But never more be officer of mine." Tied to these words came the untying of the sash of office, as Cassio was publicly stripped of his rank. Iago's face betrayed not a single emotion, if anything, his outward appearance was appalled. Inside his mind's eye though, he danced with the devil in the pale moonlight.

And with that, the axe fell.

Desdemona entered at that precise moment, drawn by the clamour, her face pale with alarm, hair down, slippers barely tied.

"Look," Othello said with regret, "if my gentle love be not raised up. I'll make thee an example."

"What's the matter?" she asked.

"All's well now, sweeting," said Othello, voice weary, "come away to bed."

He turned to Montano, still upright though ghostly. "Sir, for your hurts, myself will be your surgeon. Lead him off."

Then to Iago: "Look with care about the town, and silence those whom this vile brawl distracted."

He offered Desdemona his arm again. "Come. 'Tis the soldier's life to have their balmy slumbers waked with strife."

And they departed, like peace leaving the room.

Only Cassio remained—shattered, disgraced—and the devil beside him, waiting with open arms.

Cassio leaned upon the balustrade as if it were the mast of a foundering ship, his face drawn in a tight grimace that mixed shame with the raw throb of regret. His fine gloves were gone, his sash crooked, his eyes bloodshot and glassy with the truth of consequence.

"Iago," he groaned, "I am hurt… past all surgery."

Iago, stepping beside him with all the concern of a physician with something else in his bag, raised his brows in false alarm. "Marry, heaven forbid!"

"Reputation, reputation, reputation!" Cassio cried, hands clawing at the air like a man grasping for a ghost. "O, I have lost my reputation! I have lost the immortal part of myself—and what remains is bestial. My reputation, Iago! My reputation!"

Iago made a show of blinking. "As I am an honest man," he said—and oh, how the stars must have snickered—"I thought you had received some bodily wound. There is more sense in that than in reputation. Reputation is an idle and most false imposition—oft got without merit, and lost without deserving. You have lost no reputation at all, unless you repute yourself such a loser."

He clapped Cassio on the shoulder. "What, man! There are ways to recover the general again. You are but now cast in his mood—a punishment more in policy than in malice. Even as one would beat his offenceless dog to affright an imperious lion. Sue to him again, and he's yours."

But Cassio, his voice now wet with bitter remorse, shook his head. "I will rather sue to be despised than to deceive so good a commander with so slight, so drunken, and so indiscreet an officer. Drunk! And speak parrot? And squabble? Swagger? Swear? And discourse fustian with one's own shadow?"

He looked up, wild-eyed. "O thou invisible spirit of wine! If thou hast no name to be known by, let us call thee devil!"

Iago snorted lightly. "What was he that you followed with your sword? What had he done to you?"

"I know not."

"Is't possible?"

"I remember… a mass of things," Cassio muttered. "But nothing distinctly. A quarrel—but nothing wherefore. O God, that men should put an enemy in their mouths to steal away their brains!"

He pressed a hand to his temple. "That we should, with joy and applause, transform ourselves into beasts!"

"Ay, but you're now well enough," Iago said. "How came you thus recovered?"

"It hath pleased the devil Drunkenness to give place to the devil Wrath. One unperfectness shows me another—to make me frankly despise myself."

"Come, come," Iago soothed, "you are too severe a moraler. As the time, the place, and the condition of this country stands, I could heartily wish this had not befallen—but since it is as it is… mend it for your own good."

Cassio's expression hardened. "I will ask him for my place again. He shall tell me I am a drunkard! Had I as many mouths as Hydra, such an answer would stop them all. To be now a sensible man, by and by a fool, and presently a beast! O strange! Every inordinate cup is unblessed, and the ingredient is a devil."

"Come, come," Iago said with a laugh. "Good wine is a good familiar creature, if it be well used. Exclaim no more against it."

He paused.

"And, good lieutenant—I think you think I love you."

Cassio looked up. "I have well approved it, sir." Then, with a blush of haunted incredulity: "I—drunk!"

"You—or any man living—may be drunk at a time," Iago shrugged. "I'll tell you what you shall do. Our general's wife is now the general. I may say so in this respect—for that he hath devoted and given up himself to the contemplation, mark, and denotement of her parts and graces."

Cassio listened—wary now, but attentive.

"Confess yourself freely to her," Iago pressed. "Importune her help to put you in your place again. She is of so free, so kind, so apt, so blessed a disposition—she holds it a vice in her goodness not to do more than she is requested."

He leaned in, lowering his voice to velvet.

"This broken joint between you and her husband—entreat her to splinter it. And my fortunes against any lay worth naming: this crack of your love shall grow stronger than it was before."

Cassio, eyes lifted with a faint hope, whispered, "You advise me well."

"I protest," said Iago, hand on heart, "in the sincerity of love and honest kindness."

"I think it freely," said Cassio. "And betimes in the morning I will beseech the virtuous Desdemona to undertake for me. I am desperate of my fortunes if they cheque me here."

"You are in the right. Good night, lieutenant; I must to the watch."

"Good night, honest Iago."

Cassio departed.

And Iago remained.

...

The torches had dwindled to red stumps. The hall, once riotous, now lay hollowed out like a gutted orchard. And still Iago stood, smiling faintly into the air.

"And what's he then that says I play the villain?" he asked the darkness. "When this advice is free I give, and honest—probal to thinking, and indeed the course to win the Moor again?"

He stepped slowly into the echo of his own words.

"For 'tis most easy the inclining Desdemona to subdue in any honest suit: she's framed as fruitful as the free elements. And then for her to win the Moor?—were't to renounce his baptism, all seals and symbols of redeemed sin, his soul is so enfetter'd to her love…"

A smile flickered.

"She may make, unmake, do what she list, even as her appetite shall play the god with his weak function."

His tone darkened—turned to iron wrapped in velvet.

"How am I then a villain to counsel Cassio to this parallel course, directly to his good? Divinity of hell!"

He turned, striding toward the courtyard.

"When devils will the blackest sins put on, they do suggest at first with heavenly shows—as I do now."

The moon glanced off his teeth.

"For whiles this honest fool plies Desdemona to repair his fortunes, and she for him pleads strongly to the Moor, I'll pour this pestilence into his ear… that she repeals him for her body's lust."

He stopped.

"And by how much she strives to do him good, she shall undo her credit with the Moor. So will I turn her virtue into pitch, and out of her own goodness make the net that shall enmesh them all."

Footsteps approached—Roderigo, limping, his coat torn, his pride worse.

"How now, Roderigo?"

"I do follow here in the chase," the fool sighed, "not like a hound that hunts, but one that fills up the cry. My money is almost spent. I've been exceedingly well cudgelled." He said these words whilst rubbing a growing lump on his head, "And I think the issue will be—I shall return to Venice with no money and a little more wit."

Iago laughed. "How poor are they that have not patience! What wound did ever heal but by degrees? We work by wit, not witchcraft—and wit depends on time."

He counted upon his fingers, as if listing debts to be collected. "Cassio hath beaten thee. And thou, by that small hurt, hast cashier'd Cassio. He's all but discharged."

He smiled again.

"Though other things grow fair against the sun, yet fruits that blossom first will first be ripe. Content thyself awhile."

The sky was paling, already ink bleeding into pearl.

"By the mass—it's morning. Pleasure and action make the hours seem short. Retire thee; go where thou art billeted. Away, I say. Thou shalt know more hereafter."

Roderigo stumbled off.

Iago stood alone once more.

"Two things are to be done," he murmured. "My wife must move for Cassio to her mistress—I'll set her on. Myself the while to draw the Moor apart… and bring him jump when he may Cassio find soliciting his wife."

He turned toward the east, where light hinted at the edge of another ruinous day.

"Ay," he whispered. "That's the way. Dull not device by coldness and delay."

And with that, the devil walked on.

ACT III

The Handkerchief and the Hook

In which trust begins to rot, love turns on itself, and the net draws tighter around a noble throat.

ACT III SCENE 1

Before the castle at Cyprus, with its sun-warped stone and mosquito-laced haze, a group of musicians stood awkwardly huddled as if guilty of some minor theft. Their instruments — a disorderly rabble of viols, reeds and wind-blown things — protruded like alien limbs from their bags and cases, which had been laid down upon the paving with a reverence usually reserved for saints or brandy.

Cassio watched them with the tender but melancholy anxiety of a man trying to engineer grace out of chaos. His doublet was wrinkled from sleep unslept, and a small clump of his hair stuck at an angle to his brow, made honest by stress and the salt air. He had not been abed — nor would he lie easy again, not until the stain upon his name had been washed with Desdemona's pity, and perhaps a second chance.

"Masters," he said, with the strained affability of one who knows himself a fool but would still be seen generous. "Play here. I'll see to your pains. Something brief — light — and bid 'Good morrow, general.'"

He nodded toward the castle's upper windows. The musicians blinked like moles pulled into sunlight. One of them — a narrow man whose lips were sunken from a lifetime of blowing into oboes — gave a delicate honk by way of tune-up. Another scraped his bow once across the string and winced as though struck by his own sound.

The music began.

It was, perhaps, not the worst performance ever rendered before a fortress.

From a side alley emerged a strange figure, whose coat flapped as though protesting the body within it. His boots were muddied by dried rain from some unseen gutter, and his cap sat on his head with the irregular dignity of a tamed rat. This was the Clown — a creature of no fixed origin, his purpose shifting according to his company. Some thought him simple, some shrewd; all agreed he was inconvenient.

He paused, blinking at the music as though it might be a swarm of bees.

"Why, masters," he croaked. "Have your instruments been in Naples, that they speak i' the nose thus?"

The oboist turned, affronted. "How, sir? How?"

The Clown leaned forward conspiratorially. "Are these, I pray you, wind-instruments?"

"Ay, marry, are they."

"O, thereby hangs a tail."

"A tale, sir?"

"Marry, sir — by many a wind-instrument that I know." He grinned, revealing teeth like misaligned gravestones.

Cassio, who had until now suffered this interruption in noble silence, stepped forward with a purse and a patient smile. "But, masters," he said, "here's money for you — and the general so likes your music that he desires you, for love's sake, to make no more noise with it."

The musicians looked at one another, uncertain whether they had been praised, paid, or expelled.

"Well, sir," said the lead, "we will not."

"If you have any music that may not be heard," said the Clown, licking the salt from his lips, "to't again. But — as they say — to hear music the general does not greatly care."

"We have none such, sir."

"Then put up your pipes in your bag. Vanish into air, like a nobleman's scruples. Away!"

The musicians gathered their things in clumsy haste, tripping over one another's instruments like clowns in a farce. As they retreated down the street, the Clown turned, brushing imaginary dust from his jerkin.

"Dost thou hear, my honest friend?" Cassio asked, still watching their retreat.

The Clown squinted. "No. I hear not your honest friend; I hear you."

"Prithee," said Cassio, offering a coin he could scarcely afford, "keep up thy quillets. There's a poor piece of gold for thee. If the gentlewoman that attends the general's wife be stirring, tell her there's one Cassio entreats her a little favour of speech. Wilt thou do this?"

"She is stirring, sir. If she will stir hither, I shall seem to notify unto her."

"Do, good my friend."

The Clown doffed his cap, revealing a crown of hair like straw left too long in a swamp. "Your servant, sir. Or if not your servant, at least your messenger. Or if not your messenger, at least someone who can carry gold and bad news with equal clumsiness."

He vanished with surprising agility.

Left alone, Cassio shifted on his feet. The morning sun, still low, cast long shadows from the ramparts — tall enough to resemble the ghosts of giants, long dead. He felt his failure as a kind of presence beside him, a twin of shame that breathed with his breath.

It was in such state that Iago found him.

"You have not been a-bed, then?" Iago asked, his tone light — almost concerned — though his eyes glittered with the satisfaction of a man observing a pot just beginning to boil.

"Why, no," said Cassio. "The day had broke before we parted." He gestured toward the door with the faint hope of exculpation. "I have made bold, Iago, to send in to your wife. My suit to her is that she will to virtuous Desdemona procure me some access."

"I'll send her to you presently," said Iago, with such apparent eagerness that one might have thought him a friend of rare devotion. "And I'll devise a mean to draw the Moor out of the way — that your converse and business may be more free."

"I humbly thank you for't." Cassio bowed. "I never knew a Florentine more kind and honest."

And so Iago went — like a spider into the beams, unseen and all the more dangerous for it.

Cassio stood again alone, fingering his gloves. The shame of the brawl still burned him like a scald on the hand — and Desdemona, who had looked upon him with such honour — such grace — to be cast away by her husband on account of a drunken quarrel! Oh fool, fool that he was! The wine had gone to his head like a thief into an unlocked room, and stolen all his hopes.

Would she see him now as just another soldier? Another man who claimed honour but collapsed when the bottle offered him its bitter kiss?

He closed his eyes, ashamed. Othello loves her — and I love him — and yet I must beg through her for the restoration of myself. If this be honour, may God help the honourable.

A voice stirred him from his reverie.

"Good morrow, good Lieutenant."

It was Emilia. Her hair was hastily bound, and her eyes bore the red rim of interrupted sleep, yet her voice was firm, her gaze steady.

"I am sorry for your displeasure," she said, "but all will sure be well. The general and his wife are talking of it. And she speaks for you stoutly."

Cassio's heart, starved of hope, leapt at this.

"The Moor replies," Emilia continued, "that he you hurt is of great fame in Cyprus and great affinity — and that in wholesome wisdom he might not but refuse you. But he protests he loves you, and needs no other suitor but his likings to take the safest occasion by the front — to bring you in again."

Cassio took her hand, more reverent than bold. "Yet I beseech you — if you think fit, or that it may be done — give me advantage of some brief discourse with Desdemona alone."

"Pray you, come in," said Emilia, glancing about. "I will bestow you where you shall have time to speak your bosom freely."

"I am much bound to you," Cassio flushed, his fingers twitched at his neck, as if loosening some imagined noose. They disappeared together into the cool shadow of the castle.

Far above them, in a room still hushed by early light, a woman turned from her mirror — and a storm began to gather.

ACT III SCENE 2

A room in the Cypriot castle. Not the grand hall where lords dined and disputes were judged, nor the private chambers veiled in silks and sighs — but a cooler, sterner place of marble and maps, where the dust smelled of saltpetre and strategy.

The shutters were drawn wide, letting in the brassy light of morning. A breeze, thick with sea-damp and gull-cry, stirred the parchment scrolls laid out across a broad oaken table. Othello stood there like a carved idol — a pillar of dark stone amid drifting veils of dust and command. He held a letter in one hand — the seal of Venice already broken — and in the other, the weight of duty.

"These letters give, Iago," he said, with a slow turn of his broad hand. "To the pilot. And by him do my duties to the senate."

He did not look up as he spoke. His voice, though firm, had lost some of its resonance. Not from weakness, but from the steady narrowing of his gaze — a gaze no longer fixed on battlefields or civic honours, but increasingly caught in the net of thought.

"That done," he added, folding the second paper precisely, "I will be walking on the works. Repair there to me."

Iago took the letters with a small bow. "Well, my good lord, I'll do't."

He turned with that practiced economy of movement — the bow of a man who could not kneel without irony — and made for the doorway. Yet he lingered a moment just within the frame, listening, observing, the letters held like feathers in his hand.

Othello lifted his eyes now to the others in the room — two gentlemen of rank, officers perhaps, their tunics clean and their expressions unreadable. Men bred to receive orders, deliver courtesies, and vanish politely.

"This fortification, gentlemen," Othello said, gesturing toward the ramparts visible beyond the open arch, "shall we see't?"

"We'll wait upon your lordship," said the elder of the pair, bowing slightly.

They moved as one toward the exit, their boots clinking softly upon the flagstones. Outside, the works awaited — a ring of stone and cannon that held the future of Cyprus in its teeth. And yet, for Othello, the fortifications that pressed hardest were no longer built of lime and rock, but rumour, glances, whispers, and that unrelenting silence in Desdemona's eyes when she could not guess the storm behind his smile.

Iago, having slipped the letters into his doublet, turned again and caught the faintest beat of hesitation in his general's stride.

"My lord," he said — gently, as if offering concern. "The sea air bites hard this morning."

Othello blinked. "Aye. Yet it cools the blood."

And with that, he stepped into the sunlight.

ACT III SCENE 3

It was early still, and the garden that lay behind the fortress walls smelt of sun-warmed herbs, damp stone, and the faint copper tang of distant cannonry. Vines clung to the masonry like old secrets, while the sea air moved listlessly through the hedges, too weary to stir the laurels. A few birds chirped tentatively, uncertain whether the new day deserved a song. The garden of the citadel lay high upon the promontory's edge, where the wind came salted and untrustworthy from the east. Below, far below, the rocks clawed out from the base of the fortress wall, their black spines slick with foam. And beyond them — stretching out like a god's indifference — the Levantine Sea, glutted with centuries of war and salt and rumour.

There, beneath a trellis grown over with honeysuckle and thorns, Desdemona stood — clothed in silk and lace. Cassio faced her, cap in hand, his posture ramrod with penitence, and at his shoulder stood

Emilia, whose expression, as always, bore the wearied stamp of one too often employed in cleaning up the wreckage of men's tempers.

"Be thou assured, good Cassio," Desdemona said, her tone neither pleading nor proud, but certain — the voice of a woman whose virtue was not ornamental but active. "I will do all my abilities in thy behalf."

Emilia nodded gravely. "Good madam, do. I warrant it grieves my husband, as if the case were his."

"O, that's an honest fellow," Desdemona replied, glancing sideways at Emilia — and here, even the most careful observer might have noticed the faintest wince twitch at the edge of the maid's mouth. "Do not doubt, Cassio, but I will have my lord and you again as friendly as you were."

Cassio bowed lower. There was a moisture at the corner of his eye that might have been dew or desperation. "Bounteous madam," he said, "whatever shall become of Michael Cassio, he's never anything but your true servant."

"I know't; I thank you. You do love my lord," she said warmly, "you have known him long; and be you well assured — he shall in strangeness stand no further off than in a polite distance."

"Ay, but lady," Cassio said, and his voice cracked slightly, "that policy may either last so long, or feed upon such nice and waterish diet, or breed itself so out of circumstance..."

He faltered, suddenly aware of the danger in his words — that policy, in Othello, might become not strategy but suspicion; not justice but jealousy.

"My general may forget my love and service."

Desdemona stepped closer, laying one hand upon her breast. "Do not doubt that. Before Emilia here, I give thee warrant of thy place. Assure thee — if I do vow a friendship, I'll perform it to the last article."

She drew herself up, a soft and gentle smile on her lips.

"My lord shall never rest. I'll watch him tame and talk him out of patience. His bed shall seem a school, his board a shrift. I'll intermingle everything he does with Cassio's suit."

Her smile grew, and there was something in it of both innocence and stubbornness.

"Therefore be merry, Cassio; for thy solicitor shall rather die than give thy cause away."

Emilia, who had watched this righteous fire kindle from a single spark, now turned her head. "Madam, here comes my lord."

Cassio started — visibly. "Madam, I'll take my leave."

"Why, stay, and hear me speak," Desdemona urged.

But Cassio, already walking backward into shadow, shook his head. "Madam, not now. I am very ill at ease — unfit for mine own purposes."

"Do your discretion," she said softly.

He bowed once more and disappeared into the arcade.

At that precise moment, from the opposite path, came Othello and Iago — the one upright and composed, the other slanted slightly forward like a man always angling for an advantage. They stepped into the garden just as Cassio melted out of it.

Iago paused. He narrowed his eyes, tilted his head like a dog scenting trouble, and murmured: "Hmm, I like not that."

Othello turned. "What dost thou say?"

"Nothing, my lord," said Iago, too quickly. "Or if — I know not what."

"Was not that Cassio parted from my wife?"

Iago allowed his brow to furrow, as though this were a puzzle beyond even his considerable wit. "Cassio, my lord! No, sure. I cannot think it — that he would steal away so guilty-like, seeing you coming."

Othello's eyes fixed upon the exit Cassio had just used, as though memory still lingered in the bricks.

"I do believe 'twas he."

Desdemona, who had stood waiting with the patience of a woman confident in her righteousness, now stepped forth like a messenger bearing glad tidings.

"How now, my lord!" she said. "I have been talking with a suitor here — a man that languishes in your displeasure."

"Who is't you mean?"

"Why, your lieutenant, Cassio."

She reached gently for his hand. "Good my lord, if I have any grace or power to move you, his present reconciliation take."

Othello made a small movement with his chin — barely a nod, but not yet a refusal.

"For if he be not one that truly loves you," Desdemona pressed, "that errs in ignorance and not in cunning, I have no judgment in an honest face. I prithee, call him back."

"Went he hence now?"

"Ay, sooth. So humbled that he hath left part of his grief with me, to suffer with him."

She reached again, and this time Othello allowed the touch — though his fingers were cool and motionless.

"Good love, call him back."

"Not now, sweet Desdemona. Some other time."

"But shall't be shortly?"

"The sooner, sweet, for you."

"Shall't be tonight at supper?"

"No, not tonight."

"To-morrow dinner, then?"

"I shall not dine at home," said Othello, eyes flicking sideways. "I meet the captains at the citadel."

"Why then, to-morrow night. Or Tuesday morn. On Tuesday noon or night, or Wednesday morn—"

Her voice quickened like a bird in flight, each offer rising higher.

"I prithee, name the time — but let it not exceed three days. In faith, he's penitent. unless, as they say, the business of war demands harsh examples even from its finest — I cannot see it as a true fault, nor worthy of so sharp a reprimand."

She stepped closer, her tone now shaded with wounded pride.

"When shall he come? Tell me, Othello. I wonder in my soul what you would ask me that I should deny, or stand so mammering on. What! Michael Cassio, that came a-wooing with you — and so many a time, when I have spoke of you dispraisingly, hath ta'en your part! To have so much to do to bring him in — trust me, I could do much."

"Prithee, no more."

Othello lifted his hand — not just to silence her, but to still the dissonance rising in his chest.

"Let him come when he will. I will deny thee nothing."

Desdemona smiled, quietly triumphant. She stepped toward him and brushed his sleeve, a gesture half intimate, half political.

"Why, this is no great request," she said. "No more than asking you to wear your gloves, or take a little broth when you're ailing — or to keep yourself warm."

She laughed softly — the sound more pleased than playful — and glanced up into his face, unaware that something vast had just shifted behind his eyes.

"Or beg you to do something that plainly serves your own interest. No — when I truly mean to test the depth of your love, you'll know it. That request will carry weight, and risk, and dread to grant."

Othello looked down at her — this creature of grace and fire, who spoke now of gloves and dinners as though they bore the same moral force as reinstating a soldier to his honour. And yet he could not help but smile. He bowed his head.

"I will deny thee nothing."

It was not merely gallantry. It was truth.

"Whereon," he added, more gently now, "I do beseech thee, grant me this — to leave me but a little to myself."

Desdemona regarded him, the light fading slightly from her brow. Then, after a pause: "Shall I deny you? No."

She turned with a dignity that owed nothing to drama.

"Farewell, my lord."

"Farewell, my Desdemona," said Othello. "I'll come to thee straight."

She nodded and turned, Emilia following behind with a quick backward glance at the men. Their footsteps faded among the gravel, then the stone. Then the silence.

Othello stood for a moment, motionless, and then murmured — not to Iago, not to God, but to the air that Desdemona had just warmed:

"Sweet puckish girl." He exhaled and smiled, despite the twist in his gut. She'd charm the stars down from heaven and never notice they were burning.

"Perdition catch my soul but I do love thee — and when I love thee not…"

His voice dropped, no longer poetic but prophetic.

"…Chaos is come again."

Behind him, Iago stirred.

"My noble lord—"

"What dost thou say, Iago?"

There was a beat — the kind that sticks in the throat like a fishbone.

"Did Michael Cassio," Iago asked, "when you woo'd my lady — know of your love?"

Othello turned, slowly. "He did — from first to last. Why dost thou ask?"

Iago spread his hands as though to apologise for some accidental shadow cast by an idle gesture.

"But for a satisfaction of my thought. No further harm."

Othello's brow darkened by a shade. "Why of thy thought, Iago?"

"I did not think he had been acquainted with her."

"O, yes. And went between us very oft."

"Indeed!"

The word came too quickly, too sharp — as if Iago had bitten it and found it bitter.

Othello narrowed his eyes. "Indeed! Ay, indeed. Discern'st thou aught in that? Is he not honest?"

Iago blinked. "Honest, my lord?"

"Honest! Ay, honest."

"For aught I know," Iago said carefully, his fingers twitching as if reaching for a veil to throw over the moment, some strip of cloth to distract himself.

"What dost thou think?"

"I think, my lord."

"Think, my lord!" Othello stepped forward now, his voice growing edged. "By heaven, he echoes me — as if there were some monster in his thought too hideous to be shown."

He moved closer still, no longer the calm general, but a man driven not by rage yet — but by something worse: curiosity.

"Thou dost mean something," he said. "I heard thee say even now, thou likedst not that — when Cassio left my wife. What didst not like?"

Iago remained still, but the tension rose in him like a bowstring pulled taut.

"And when I told thee he was of my counsel in my whole course of wooing, thou criedst 'Indeed!' and didst purse thy brow together — as if thou then hadst shut up in thy brain some horrible conceit. If thou dost love me, show me thy thought."

There was a silence. Even the gulls had stopped crying.

"My lord," Iago said, at length, "you know I love you."

"I think thou dost."

Othello's voice was quiet now — not from calm, but from weight.

"And, for I know thou'rt full of love and honesty, and weigh'st thy words before thou givest them breath — therefore these stops of thine fright me the more. For such things in a false, disloyal knave are tricks of custom. But in a man that's just…"

He paused.

"They are secret denunciations— working from the heart that passion cannot rule."

Iago lowered his gaze, as if ashamed to meet the truth of what he must now say — or pretend not to.

"For Michael Cassio," he said slowly, "I dare be sworn I think that he is honest."

"I think so too," said Othello — but there was a war already under way between the parts of him that answered.

"Men should be what they seem," said Iago, the line falling from his lips like doctrine behind his own mask. "Or those that be not what they seem, should not try to seem so."

"Certain, men should be what they seem," Othello echoed — but his words had begun to hollow, like wood softened by rot.

"Why, then," said Iago, "I think Cassio's an honest man."

Othello drew a breath. "Nay — yet there's more in this."

He stepped closer still. They were near enough now that their voices could not carry far. The air was still and sharp.

"I prithee, speak to me as to thy thinkings — as thou dost ruminate — and give thy worst of thoughts the worst of words."

"Good my lord," said Iago, hands raised in apology, "pardon me. Though I am bound to every act of duty, I am not bound to that all slaves are free to. Utter my thoughts? Why — say they are vile and false."

He stepped away, then turned, as if the argument were now with himself as much as with Othello.

Tell me — what palace stands so pure that no filth has ever found its way in? Whose heart is so spotless that some dark suspicion hasn't sat down there, uninvited, and held quiet trial beside nobler thoughts?

"Thou dost conspire against thy friend, Iago," Othello said, his voice beginning to quake — not in anger, not yet, but in dread.

"If thou but think'st him wrong'd, and makest his ear a stranger to thy thoughts…"

"I do beseech you—" Iago began, then broke off. His next words came halting, reluctant.

"Though I perchance am vicious in my guess — as, I confess, it is my nature's plague to spy into abuses, and oft my jealousy shapes faults that are not — that your wisdom yet, from my own imperfect understanding, would take no notice…"

He looked up.

"Nor build yourself a trouble out of his scattering and unsure observance. It were not for your quiet, nor your good, nor for my manhood, honesty, or wisdom, to let you know my thoughts."

Othello stared at him. "What dost thou mean?"

And now Iago turned slowly, eyes gleaming with sincerity too real to be trusted.

"Good name in man and woman, dear my lord, is the immediate jewel of their souls."

He placed one hand upon his chest, like a priest preparing to absolve or accuse.

"Who steals my purse steals trash. 'Tis something, nothing. 'Twas mine, 'tis his, and has been slave to thousands."

His eyes locked with Othello's, and now his voice dropped — deeper, darker.

"But he that filches from me my good name robs me of that which not enriches him…"

A pause.

"…and makes me poor indeed."

"By heaven, I'll know thy thoughts," said Othello.

His voice, though low, cut through the garden like a blade through cloth. Somewhere above, a dove scattered from its perch with a flutter of wings too loud for peace.

Iago turned slowly — not startled, but as though considering the right shape for refusal.

"You cannot," he said, "if my heart were in your hand. Nor shall not, whilst 'tis in my custody."

"Ha?" The sound from Othello's throat was not a word — not quite. It was the bark of a man pushed from the edge of certainty into the gulf of fear.

And then, like oil onto fire, Iago dropped the most famous bait in the canon of betrayal:

"O, beware, my lord, of jealousy." He paused, rueful. "It is the green-eyed monster which doth mock the meat it feeds on."

He said it like a proverb handed down from Hell.

"That cuckold lives in bliss who, certain of his fate, loves not his wronger. But O — what damned minutes tells he o'er, who dotes, yet doubts… suspects, yet strongly loves!"

Othello's breath hissed between his teeth. "O misery!"

"Poor and content," said Iago, gently now, as though he were offering comfort rather than unmaking a man, "is rich, and rich enough. but the man who has everything, and lives in dread of losing it — he's poorer than winter."

He placed a hand to his breast. "Good heaven, the souls of all my tribe defend from jealousy."

"Why — why is this?" Othello demanded. "Think'st thou I'd make a lie of jealousy — to follow still the changes of the moon with fresh suspicions? No."

His voice cracked with the effort to remain rational. "To be once in doubt is once to be resolved. Exchange me for a goat when I shall turn the business of my soul to such puffed and blown surmises, matching thy inference."

He was pacing now, short steps back and forth, hands half-raised like a man trying to push back a rising wave.

"'Tis not to make me jealous to say my wife is fair, has a good appetite, loves company, speaks freely, sings, plays, and dances well. Where virtue is, these are more virtuous."

He stopped, turned, and held up a hand as if swearing an oath.

"Nor from mine own weak merits will I draw the smallest fear or doubt of her revolt. For she had eyes, and chose me. No, Iago."

A pause. A dying flicker of light.

"I'll see before I doubt; when I doubt, prove; and on the proof, there is no more but this: away at once with love or jealousy."

Iago let the moment hang. And then, with careful gravity: "I am glad of it. For now I shall have reason to show the love and duty that I bear you with franker spirit."

He stepped closer, lowering his voice. "Therefore, as I am bound, receive it from me. I speak not yet of proof. Look to your wife. Observe her well with Cassio. Wear your eye thus — not jealous, nor secure."

129

A pause. The voice that followed was nearly tender:

"I would not have your free and noble nature, out of self-bounty, be abused. Look to't."

He turned aside, as if speaking half to himself. "I know our country disposition well. In Venice, they do let heaven witness the games they wouldn't dare show their husbands. Their virtue isn't in leaving something undone... but keeping it unknown."

"Dost thou say so?" Othello whispered. His foreignness had often earned him admiration as the noble outsider, the exotic general. But it also kept certain doors forever closed, and behind those doors, *prejudices grew fat in the dark*, murmured in salons and boudoirs where skin was white and blood blue.

"She did deceive her father, marrying you," said Iago, looking up slowly. "And when she seem'd to shake and fear your looks, she loved them most."

Othello nodded, faintly. "And so she did."

"Why, go to then." Iago's voice became gentle, persuasive — as if Othello had only just now reached the beginning of wisdom.

"She that, so young, could give out such a seeming — to seal her father's eyes up close as oak... He thought 'twas witchcraft..."

He paused. Then, with a low bow: "But I am much to blame. I humbly do beseech you of your pardon — for too much loving you."

Othello looked at him, eyes no longer burning but glassy, stunned. "I am bound to thee for ever."

Iago watched him with narrowed eyes. That was the moment. The hook set. The blood changed colour. The silence stretched uncounted for several turns. Only the sound of the sea remained indifferent to the tension.

"I see this hath a little dash'd your spirits," Iago said.

"Not a jot. Not a jot."

But Othello's voice was hollow now — the kind of lie a man tells when his heart has dropped through the floor and he cannot bear the sound it made hitting the bottom.

"In faith, I fear it has," said Iago, with the mock-anxiety of a man testing a wound he himself inflicted. "I hope you will consider what is spoke comes from my love. But I do see you're moved."

Othello's jaw twitched.

"I am to pray you not to strain my speech to grosser issues, nor to larger reach, than to suspicion."

"I will not."

"Should you do so, my lord," Iago continued smoothly, "my speech should fall into such vile success as my thoughts aim not at. Cassio's my worthy friend— My lord, I see you're moved."

"No — not much moved," said Othello. "I do not think but Desdemona's honest."

"Long live she so," said Iago, with mock-benignity, "and long live you to think so."

Iago once again let silence be the hammer that drove deeper the nails he had lined up.

"And yet," said Othello slowly, "how nature erring from itself—"

"Ay, there's the point," said Iago, jumping on it. "To be bold with you — women, like all creatures, tend toward matches of their own kind. Their own clime. Their own colour. Their own class. In all things, nature leans toward likeness — and when it does not, well…"

He gave a derisive snort, gesturing broadly with a sweep of hand and brow. "Foh! One may smell in such a will most rank, foul disproportion, thoughts unnatural."

Then, as if realising he had pushed too far:

"But pardon me. I do not in position distinctly speak of her. Only… it may be that her heart, sobered by time and judgment, will turn back toward her own… and come to repent the match she made"

Othello raised his hand, but it no longer commanded. It trembled slightly, his body beginning to betray his soul.

"Farewell, farewell."

His voice was not the voice of a general now. It was the voice of a man who had begun to see ghosts in sunlight.

"If more thou dost perceive, let me know more. Set on thy wife to observe. Leave me, Iago."

Iago bowed, began to turn. He took three quick steps away, but the muscles on his face were already tensing into a grin when —

"Why did I marry?" Othello asked aloud. Not to him. Not to anyone.

"This honest creature doubtless sees and knows more — much more — than he unfolds."

Iago returned, gentle as silk.

"My lord, I would you were content to scan this thing no further; leave it to time. Though it be fit that Cassio have his place — for sure, he fills it up with great ability — yet, if you please to hold him off awhile, you shall by that perceive him and his means."

He placed a final, strategic feather on the scale.

"Watch her," his voice falling to a murmur. "See how earnestly she presses you to take him back. If her pleading turns sharp, insistent — well, there'll be much to learn in that alone."

Then he bowed — a gesture polished enough for court, and subtle enough for a gallows.

"Let me be judged too anxious, if you will," he said. "For I have cause to fear — and fear I do. But until proof strikes home, I hold her free. That, I do most humbly swear to your honour.

Othello said nothing, but his hands opened and closed at his sides like the clenching of a vice.

"Fear not my government," he muttered.

"I once more take my leave," said Iago.

And he left — the garden still behind him, but the garden of Othello's soul now darkened utterly. He stood quite still beneath the orange tree. The sun had passed its zenith, casting long shadows through the garden. Bees moved drunkenly between the flowers, oblivious to the wars waged in human hearts.

"This fellow's of exceeding honesty…"

Othello's mind gnawed upon the phrase, again and again, as though by repetition it might resolve into something safer. Iago — honest

Iago — was no fool. He had seen things. He had not seen things. His very reluctance was a kind of confirmation.

"And knows all qualities, with a learned spirit, of human dealings…"

He frowned, staring into the gravel. His hand flexed at his side. His heart — that strong heart which had borne storms and sieges, stood before cannon and plague — now trembled over the unfathomable.

"If I do prove her haggard…"

The falconry image rose unbidden: a wild bird once hooded and leashed, now wheeling free above his reach.

"Though her jesses were my dear heartstrings, I'd whistle her off and let her down the wind — to prey at fortune…"

That was justice, was it not? To let her go. But justice is no balm for love, only a blade for it. And still — the thought returned, ugly, irresistible.

"Haply, for I am black…"

The words came like knives from his own mouth, unspoken yet cutting. He had always known the murmurs. Had laughed at them. But here — in the stillness of this garden — they echoed louder than cannon fire.

"And have not those soft parts of conversation that chamberers have…Or am I declined into the vale of years…"

He clenched his fists.

"Yet that's not much. And still — the worst part: She's gone."

It was not accusation now. It was lament.

"I am abused. And my relief... must be to loathe her."

He stood there, not breathing, as though some internal war had stilled every bodily function but thought. Behind his eyes, a monstrous vision was forming — and yet it refused full shape. A shadow, shifting.

"O curse of marriage..."

He thought of their wedding night. Of fingers trembling on laces. Of skin uncovered, not for conquest, but for communion.

"That we can call these delicate creatures ours — and not their appetites!"

He staggered a step forward, caught himself.

"I had rather be a toad, and live upon the vapour of a dungeon, than keep a corner in the thing I love for others' uses..."

He felt sick. Not only with suspicion, but with self-hatred. How did I come to this?

"Yet 'tis the plague of great ones... power grants no pardon from betrayal...."

He looked up — and for a moment, saw nothing but gold light and green leaves. Then —

"'Tis destiny unshunnable, like death..."

A rustle of fabric behind him. He turned his head, and there she was.

She came into the light with a grace that seemed almost unreal, the silk of her gown catching sun like fishscale. Her hair, unbound for the midday heat, floated around her like a halo in a religious icon. And Othello — in that moment — stood so still, so knotted in muscular anguish, that Desdemona saw him as though carved from stone.

135

He reminded her — absurdly, perfectly — of a statue she had admired in her girlhood on a visit to Florence: Hercules and Nessus, locked in battle, the hero seizing the treacherous centaur as it tried to carry off his bride. All sinew and struggle, all burden and betrayal. And yet it was not rage in Othello's face. It was confusion. And pain.

She stepped forward gently.

"If she be false," Othello thought — or prayed — then heaven mocks itself.

And aloud — not to her, but the universe: "I'll not believe't."

"How now, my dear Othello?"

Her voice was light, concerned. No edge, no cunning. Her face an open sky.

"Your dinner, and the generous islanders by you invited, do attend your presence."

He blinked, as if returning from a dream. "I am to blame."

"Why do you speak so faintly? Are you not well?"

There was a pause. Then he touched his forehead.

"I have a pain… upon my forehead here."

She smiled — relieved, thinking it some passing illness. "'Faith, that's with watching. 'Twill away again. Let me but bind it hard — within this hour it will be well."

She reached for her handkerchief — that small square of fine white linen embroidered in red strawberries — and pressed it gently to his brow.

He flinched.

"Your napkin is too little," he said, and brushed her hand aside. In the motion, the handkerchief fluttered from her grasp and fell to the stones between them.

"Let it alone," he said. "Come, I'll go in with you."

She looked down at the cloth, puzzled, then back up at him — his tone too curt, too clipped. But he was already turning.

"I am very sorry that you are not well," she said. She bent to retrieve her precious handkerchief, and hastily stuffed it in her sleeve as she chased her love. A light breeze from across the ocean, perhaps a butterfly flapping its wings in distant Asia turned now into something barely enough to lift a feather, dislodged the cloth again and it floated down to the ground behind her.

And they walked hurriedly away, the handkerchief lying still in the garden — white as innocence, red as betrayal.

...

Emilia found it lying where the shadows of the arcade crossed the path — the delicate square of white linen, just faintly dusted from the ground. She bent and picked it up carefully, brushing it with the heel of her palm.

The embroidered red strawberries — no larger than a fingernail each — had been worked in silk so fine they seemed to float upon the cloth like real fruit. She knew this handkerchief well. It was the first remembrance the Moor had given Desdemona — and the only one she carried always. Emilia had seen her press it to her lips, fold it lovingly into her bodice, speak to it in moments of solitude like a child whispering to a relic of her mother.

Emilia frowned. She should return it at once.

And yet…

My wayward husband hath a hundred times woo'd me to steal it.

It was true. Iago had asked for it — half in jest, half in some obscure desire he never fully explained. Always, she had refused him. But now? It had not been stolen, not truly. It had been dropped. A woman can pick up what the wind has claimed — and choose to place it elsewhere.

I'll have the work ta'en out, and give't Iago…

She turned it once more in her hand. Heaven knows what he will do with it, she thought, not I. I nothing but to please his fantasy.

The gate creaked behind her.

"How now!" said Iago, his boots scuffing the gravel. "What do you here alone?"

She turned, startled. "Do not you chide. I have a thing for you."

"A thing for me?" he sneered, raising a brow. "It is a common thing—"

"Ha!" she snapped, with sudden fire.

"To have a foolish wife," he finished, dryly.

"Oh — is that all?" she said coolly, and held up the handkerchief between two fingers. "What will you give me now for the same handkerchief?"

"What handkerchief?"

"What handkerchief?" she repeated, incredulous. "Why, that the Moor first gave to Desdemona — that which so often you did bid me steal."

138

His eyes flared. "Hast stolen it from her?"

"No, in faith. She let it drop by negligence. And, to the advantage — I, being here, took it up. Look — here it is."

He stepped forward. "A good wench. Give it me."

"What will you do with it, that you have been so earnest to have me filch it?"

She held it just beyond his grasp — but not with resistance, only question.

Iago reached. "Give it me."

"If it be not for some purpose of import…" she began.

"Give it me!" He snatched it from her, so roughly the linen twisted in his fingers.

Emilia flinched. She knew that quick violence of his, it was both the expression of his passion and of his shame. "Poor lady — she'll run mad when she shall lack it."

"Be not acknown on it," he muttered. "I have use for it. Go — leave me."

She stood for a moment longer, then turned and went — her shadow trailing behind like a tattered conscience.

When she had gone, Iago held the handkerchief up to the light. The white fabric shimmered like innocence itself, and the strawberries — red, perfect — seemed almost wet.

"I will in Cassio's lodging lose this napkin," he said aloud, eyes narrowing. "And let him find it."

His tone changed — colder now, almost scholarly.

"Trifles light as air are, to the jealous, confirmations strong as proofs of holy writ."

He turned the cloth slowly in his fingers, as though measuring the exact weight of its symbolism.

"This may do something. The Moor already changes with my poison. Dangerous conceits are, in their natures, poisons — which at the first are scarce found to distaste, but with a little act upon the blood... burn like the mines of sulphur."

He tucked the cloth into his doublet.

"I did say so."

A sound behind him. Iago turned.

"Look, where he comes."

And Othello entered.

His gait was slower now. Not from age, but from the effort of containing something vast and corrosive. He looked like a man walking across a battlefield made of his own thoughts.

Iago smiled.

"Not poppy, nor mandragora, nor all the drowsy syrups of the world, shall ever medicine thee to that sweet sleep thou owedst yesterday."

"Ha! ha!" Othello barked, with no mirth. "False to me?"

Iago raised his hands in gentle protest. "Why, how now, general? No more of that."

"Avaunt!" cried Othello. "Be gone! Thou hast set me on the rack. I swear — 'tis better to be much abused than but to know't a little."

"How now, my lord?"

"What sense had I of her stolen hours of lust?"

Othello was no longer speaking to Iago, he was angry at the universe.

"I saw't not, thought it not, it harm'd not me. I slept the next night well, was free and merry. I found not Cassio's kisses on her lips!"

He turned sharply.

"He that is robbed, not wanting what is stolen, let him not know't — and he's not robbed at all."

Iago, quietly, "I am sorry to hear this."

"I had been happy," Othello said, and his voice cracked — not with rage now, but something far closer to grief. "If the general camp — even the lowest pioneers and all — had tasted her sweet body, so I had nothing known…"

And then the death of him, spoken aloud:

"O, now, forever farewell the tranquil mind! Farewell content! Farewell the plumed troop, and the big wars, that make ambition virtue!"

His voice rose now, terrifying in its beauty.

"O, farewell! Farewell the neighing steed and the shrill trump, the spirit-stirring drum, the ear-piercing fife — the royal banner, and all quality, pride, pomp, and circumstance of glorious war!"

He looked up at the sky, chest heaving. Beyond the garden wall, the Levantine Sea battered the cliff face in its ancient, indifferent march, waves slapping the rocks below like some slow applause for ruin. For a moment, Iago feared he would leap — cast himself down into the breakers and let them swallow what was left.

"And, O you mortal engines, whose rude throats the immortal Jove's dead clamours counterfeit — farewell!"

Othello touched his chest — and for the first time seemed to feel the full weight of his ruin.

"Othello's occupation's gone."

He took a staggering step toward the edge —

— and Iago caught him.

"Is't possible, my lord?" he asked gently, keeping hold of the man, as though steadying a brother… or preparing a puppet.

Othello's spun around, eyes flared. "Villain — be sure thou prove my love a whore. Be sure of it. Give me the ocular proof."

He stepped forward now, thunder beneath his voice.

"Or by the worth of man's eternal soul — thou hadst been better have been born a dog than answer my waked wrath!"

"Is't come to this?" said Iago, recoiling half a step — no longer restraining his general but reeling in his prey.

"Make me to see't," Othello growled. "Or at the least so prove it, that the probation bear no hinge nor loop to hang a doubt on — or woe upon thy life!"

"My noble lord—"

"If thou dost slander her and torture me," said Othello, trembling now, "never pray more. Abandon all remorse. On horror's head, horrors accumulate. Do deeds to make heaven weep, all earth amazed — for nothing canst thou to damnation add greater than that."

Iago staggered back, hands up like a prophet burdened with vision.

"O grace! O heaven forgive me! Are you a man? Have you a soul or sense? God be wi' you — take mine office. O wretched fool that livest to make thine honesty a vice!"

He turned from Othello and cried aloud:

"O monstrous world! Take note, take note, O world — to be direct and honest is not safe."

He bowed mockingly, his voice bitter with feigned pain.

"I thank you for this profit. And from hence, I'll love no friend, since love breeds such offence."

"Nay — stay," Othello said. His voice was quieter now, strangled by the chaos swelling behind his ribs. "Thou shouldst be honest."

"I should be wise," said Iago coldly. "For honesty's a fool — and loses that it works for."

Othello raised a shaking hand.

"By the world… I think my wife be honest, and think she is not. I think that thou art just, and think thou art not."

He took a breath, as if drowning. Iago stood motionless, stony.

"I'll have some proof. Her name — that was as fresh as Dian's visage — is now begrimed and black as mine own face."

He turned, his hands balled into fists.

"If there be cords, or knives, poison, or fire, or suffocating streams — I'll not endure it."

He bent forward slightly, as if the weight of his thoughts had become corporeal.

"Would I were satisfied!"

Iago's eyes lit now with perfect control.

"I see, sir, you are eaten up with passion. I do repent me that I put it to you."

Othello stared at him.

"You would be satisfied?"

"Would?" Othello barked. "Nay — I will."

"And may. But how? How satisfied, my lord?"

He tilted his head — predator masking as priest.

"Would you, the supervisor, grossly gape on — behold her topp'd?"

"Death and damnation! O!" Othello roared.

"It would be a tedious difficulty, I think," said Iago calmly, "to bring them to that prospect."

He gestured with both hands, the full crudity of his image spelled out with the sounds of intercourse.

"Damn them then, if ever mortal eyes do see them bolster more than their own. What then? How then? Where's satisfaction? 'Tis impossible you should see this."

His tone shifted now to brutal parody.

"Were they as prime as goats, as hot as monkeys, as salt as wolves in pride — and fools as gross as ignorance made drunk. But yet — I say — if imputation and strong circumstances, which lead directly to the door of truth, will give you satisfaction — you may have't."

Othello clenched his jaw.

"Give me a living reason she's disloyal."

Iago sighed. "I do not like the office."

He glanced aside, as if loathing what he must say.

"But since I am entered in this cause so far, prick'd to't by foolish honesty and love… I will go on."

He leaned close, voice dropping.

"I lay with Cassio lately, my Fair Lord." Iago began his tale with a soft, low voice. In wartime, even officers sometimes shared a bed — aboard ship, or in a garrison where room was tight and comfort rarer still. But Iago offered no such explanation. He let the words do their dark work. He continued "And being troubled with a raging tooth, I could not sleep."

Othello said nothing.

"There are a kind of men," Iago continued, "so loose of soul, that in their sleeps will mutter their affairs. One of this kind is Cassio."

He took a single step closer. His voice, low and languid now, took on the rhythm of a confessional.

"In sleep I heard him say — 'Sweet Desdemona, let us be wary, let us hide our loves.'" His voice mimicked the soft moaning of a lover.

145

Iago lifted one hand, miming the ghost of a caress. Then his other hand followed, and he mimed being gripped — too tight — his own wrist enclosed in an invisible embrace.

"And then, sir — would he gripe and wring my hand, cry 'O sweet creature!' — and then kiss me hard —"

He leaned in. His lips did not touch Othello, but his breath did.

"— as if he pluck'd up kisses by the roots that grew upon my lips."

He ran his tongue briefly across his own mouth.

"Then laid his leg… over my thigh…"

His voice dropped, intimate now, husky.

"…and sigh'd. And kiss'd. And then cried — 'Cursed fate that gave thee to the Moor!'"

He turned his face away — too suddenly, too neatly. The performance had become a little too real.

Othello staggered back, his face contorted, not just with fury but with revulsion, confusion — something for which he had no language.

"O monstrous! Monstrous!"

"Nay — this was but his dream," said Iago sweetly, as if to soothe a child waking from nightmare.

But Othello's voice was thick with horror. "But this — denoted a foregone conclusion. 'Tis a shrewd doubt, though it be but a dream."

Iago nodded, voice steady again, slipping back into command. "And this may help to thicken other proofs that do demonstrate thinly."

"I'll tear her all to pieces!"

"Nay, but be wise," Iago murmured, the chessboard before him in his mind. "We see nothing done. She may be honest yet. Tell me but this—"

He shifted now to a new piece.

"Have you not sometimes seen a handkerchief — spotted with strawberries — in your wife's hand?"

Othello froze. His body stiffened as if turned to marble.

"I gave her such a one. 'Twas my first gift."

"I know not that," said Iago, feigning distance. "But such a handkerchief — I am sure it was your wife's — did I today see Cassio wipe his beard with."

Othello turned to stone.

"If it be that…"

"If it be that, or any that was hers," said Iago, "it speaks against her with the other proofs."

Othello's hands shook violently.

"O — that the slave had forty thousand lives! One is too poor, too weak for my revenge."

He thrust his arms toward the sky.

"Now do I see 'tis true! Look here, Iago — all my fond love thus do I blow to heaven!"

He clapped his hands together.

"'Tis gone. Arise, black vengeance, from thy hollow cell!"

He placed a palm upon his heart.

"Yield up, O love, thy crown and hearted throne — to tyrannous hate! Swell, bosom, with thy fraught — for 'tis of aspics' tongues!"

"O, blood, blood, blood!" he cried.

"Patience," Iago said, though he smiled now. "Your mind perhaps may change."

"Never, Iago! Like to the Pontic sea, whose icy current and compulsive course ne'er feels retiring ebb, but keeps due on to the Propontic and the Hellespont — even so my bloody thoughts, with violent pace, shall ne'er look back, ne'er ebb to humble love, till that a capable and wide revenge swallow them up!"

He fell to one knee.

"Now, by yond marble heaven, in the due reverence of a sacred vow — I here engage my words."

"Do not rise yet," said Iago.

He knelt beside his general.

"Witness, you ever-burning lights above, you elements that clip us round about, witness that here Iago doth give up the execution of his wit, hands, heart, to wrong'd Othello's service!"

He placed a hand upon his breast.

"Let him command. And to obey shall be in me remorse — what bloody business ever."

They rose.

Othello turned to him.

"I greet thy love — not with vain thanks, but with acceptance bounteous. And will upon the instant put thee to't. Within three days let me hear thee say that Cassio's not alive."

"My friend is dead," Iago replied. "'Tis done at your request."

Then — with one final feint of mercy: "But let her live."

"Damn her, lewd minx! O, damn her!" Othello spat.

"Come, go with me apart. I will withdraw, to furnish me with some swift means of death for the fair devil."

He looked now with pure, fixed purpose.

"Now art thou my lieutenant."

And Iago — bowing low, with a smile that only the gods could see — whispered:

"I am your own forever."

ACT III SCENE 4

The garden was quieter now — the air heavy, the light beginning to take on that late-Cypriot burnish, as if the sun itself had tired of the heat it spilled. By the gate, Desdemona paced, distracted, her hands fluttering like leaves disturbed by wind.

"Do you know, sirrah," she said to the loitering Clown, "where Lieutenant Cassio lies?"

The Clown blinked at her with bright, meaningless eyes. "I dare not say he lies anywhere," he said gravely.

Desdemona frowned. "Why, man?"

"He's a soldier," said the Clown with a small bow. "And to say a soldier lies is to stab at his honour — and I'm unarmed, madam."

Emilia rolled her eyes. Desdemona, not in the mood for riddles, pressed on.

"Where lodges he?"

"To tell you where he lodges," said the Clown with mock solemnity, "is to tell you where I lie."

"Can anything be made of this?" she muttered.

"Madam, I know not where he sleeps — and for me to conjure up a bed and say he lies there, would be to lie in mine own throat." He clutched his neck, as if to protect the honesty inside it.

Desdemona gave a breathless laugh and waved him off. "Can you inquire him out, and be edified by report?"

"I shall catechise the world for him," said the Clown, as if embarking on pilgrimage. "That is, ask questions — and from them find answers."

"Then seek him," she said. "Tell him I have moved my lord for him — and that I hope all shall be well."

He bowed. "To do this is within the compass of man's wit. And therefore, I will attempt it."

He vanished through the gate, whistling something off-key.

Emilia gave her mistress a glance that lingered too long. "Where should I lose that handkerchief?" Desdemona said quietly, voice troubled now that the Clown had gone. "Emilia, do you know?"

"I know not, madam."

"I'd rather have lost my purse full of crusadoes," Desdemona murmured. "And but that my noble Moor is true of mind, and made of no such baseness as jealous creatures are…" She faltered. "Still — it would be enough to put him to ill thinking."

Emilia watched her carefully. "Is he not jealous?"

Desdemona shook her head, too quickly. "Who, he? No. I think the sun where he was born drew all such humours out of him." She smiled — a brave smile, brittle as glass.

Emilia opened her mouth, then closed it again. Her silence felt heavier than any warning.

Just then, the gate swung open — and Othello entered.

Desdemona straightened, smoothing her gown. "I will not leave him now till Cassio be call'd to him," she whispered.

"How is't with you, my lord?" she called gently.

Othello's face was unreadable. "Well, my good lady," he said.

But inwardly, he burned.

O, hardness to dissemble, he thought. To speak soft when the blood claps in the ears...To look upon her and not see the ghost of the lie I fear...

"How do you, Desdemona?"

"Well, my good lord," she replied, puzzled by the hollowness in his tone.

"Give me your hand," he said. Then paused.

"This hand is moist, my lady."

She laughed softly. "It yet hath felt no age nor known no sorrow."

"This argues fruitfulness," he said, examining it with something like suspicion. "And a liberal heart. Hot. Hot and moist. This hand of yours requires sequester from liberty — fasting, prayer, much castigation.

For here's a young and sweating devil, that commonly rebels. 'Tis a good hand... a frank one."

"You may indeed say so," she said. "'Twas that hand that gave away my heart."

He smiled, though the smile never touched his eyes. "A liberal hand. The hearts of old gave hands — but now our new heraldry is hands, not hearts."

Desdemona looked at him. "I cannot speak of this. Come now, your promise."

"What promise, chuck?"

She frowned at the term. "I have sent to bid Cassio come speak with you."

Othello turned away. "I have a salt and sorry rheum that offends me." Then, still not looking at her: "Lend me thy handkerchief."

She reached for her sleeve. "Here, my lord."

He turned to her.

"That which I gave you."

Her hand faltered. "I have it not about me."

He froze. "Not?"

"No, indeed, my lord," she said gently, still thinking the matter slight. Her worry that she had misplaced it could not escape her eyes, but Othello read that innocent regret as something sly, dishonest. Othello did not move. Something cracked within him — not loudly, but with the awful softness of fabric tearing along its seams.

"That is a fault."

And now his voice lowered — deeper than she'd heard it, not loud but vast, like an oath spoken into the vault of a tomb.

"That handkerchief... did an Egyptian to my mother give. She was a charmer — she could read the thoughts of people." These words, Othello spoke deep into Desdemona's eyes, as though he too could read her thoughts. "She told her that, while she kept it, it would make her loved and keep her husband bound to her. But if she lost it... or made gift of it... his love would rot. His spirit would stray." Othello here paused and took a calming breath.

"She, dying, gave it me. And bade me, when my fate would have me wive, to give it her. I did so."

His eyes were fixed on her now.

"Take heed on't. Keep it like your precious eye. To lose it... or give it away... were such perdition as nothing else could match."

Desdemona swallowed. "Is't possible?"

"'Tis true," Othello said at last, his voice thick and low, like oil running over stone. "There's magic in the web of it."

Desdemona blinked, not understanding.

"A sibyl," he continued, "a woman past two hundred in her reckonings of the sun, sewed it in the furies of prophecy. The worms that spun the silk were hallow'd, and the dye—dyed in mummy, preserved from the hearts of dead maidens."

He turned toward her then, and the light caught on the scar above his brow, accentuating the hollows of his cheeks. His face, once noble, bore now the look of something chiselled from grief.

154

"Indeed?" said Desdemona, a soft tremor in her voice. "Is't true?"

"Most veritable," he replied. "Therefore look to't well."

And here, something shifted. It passed between them like the gust before a storm. Desdemona flinched, as if struck not by hand but by foreboding.

"Then would to God," she whispered, eyes shining with confusion, "that I had never seen't."

He turned sharply.

"Ha! Wherefore?"

Her hands clasped together, her voice rising a pitch. "Why do you speak so suddenly—so rashly?"

Othello advanced a step, the air around him growing taut. "Is't lost?" he demanded. "Gone? Speak—has it strayed out of your keeping?"

Desdemona stared, her mouth parting in helplessness. "Heaven bless us!"

"Say you?" he barked.

"It is not lost," she insisted, half rising. "But—what if it were?"

"How?" His voice was hollow now, the echo of a man unravelling. "What?"

"I say, it is not lost."

"Fetch it," said he, and the command struck the room like a bell tolling from the gallows. "Let me see't."

"I could," she answered with unsteady patience, "but not now. This is a trick to put me from my suit—please, my lord, let Cassio be received again."

He froze. A line of sweat coursed down the side of his face, vanishing into his collar. His thoughts, coiled and venomous, turned upon her plea like a snake upon an intruder.

"Fetch me the handkerchief," he said again, quieter this time. "My mind misgives."

"Come, come," Desdemona urged, her voice lilting with hope, "you'll never meet a man more sufficient, more loyal—"

"The handkerchief!" he roared.

The chamber quivered. A pigeon beyond the shutter startled and took flight.

"I pray you," she pleaded, "talk to me of Cassio—"

"The handkerchief!" he thundered, like the moan of thunder from a gathering cloud.

Her hands flew up. "A man who has spent his fortunes on your love! Who has shared your dangers—"

"The handkerchief!" His words now were weapons, each syllable hurled with the finality of a sentence passed.

She staggered back, wilting under his fury. "In sooth, my lord, you are to blame—"

"Away!" he cried, and flung himself from the chamber.

The door slammed shut behind him. Silence fell, and in it, the disarrayed lace of Desdemona's sleeve fluttered like a wounded moth.

She stood alone now, left to collect the remnants of a love that had begun to smoke and curl, like parchment cast too near a flame.

She moved not. The room seemed smaller now, suffocating in its hush. Through the closed window, a breeze carried the scent of brine and olives, a sharpness that caught in the throat—a world still turning, yet somehow more hostile.

Far away in the market square, a bell tolled for the hour. But here, it tolled for something else. Something lost. Something unravelled. Something that, once vanished, could never be sewn again. Emilia watched Desdemona with an expression that might have seemed idle to a stranger, but beneath her gentlewoman's eyes there churned an old bitterness, too familiar to be spoken aloud. She crossed to her mistress and, without asking, adjusted the lace upon her shoulder with a care half maternal, half resigned.

"Is not this man jealous?" she said in a tone stripped of wonder, as though jealousy in men were as common and natural as the sea wind.

Desdemona, eyes troubled as storm-lit glass, shook her head slowly. "I ne'er saw this before," she whispered. "There's… some wonder in that handkerchief. I am most unhappy in the loss of it."

And indeed she looked it—her countenance pale as mourning silk, her form heavy with a grief that had not yet named itself but seemed already to fill the room like a rising flood.

Emilia gave a mirthless breath. "'Tis not a year or two shows us a man," she said, more to the air than her lady. "They're all but stomachs, and we all but food; they eat us hungerly, and when full, they belch us."

She paused, seeing movement beyond the columned veranda. "Look you," she added, pointing. "Cassio and my husband."

Sure enough, up the path strode Iago with his careful ease, that feline swiftness of purpose masked by affable gait, and beside him the pale figure of Cassio, humble but resolute, clutching his hat like a condemned man grasping his own pardon.

"There is no other way," Iago said, his tone oily with encouragement. "'Tis she must do it. And lo, the happiness—go now, and importune her."

Cassio bowed low. "Madam," he began, "my former suit—"

Desdemona offered a tired smile that barely lifted the corners of her mouth. "How now, good Cassio?"

"I do beseech you," he said, his voice rich with sincerity, "that by your virtuous means I may again exist—be counted once more among the favoured of him whom I so dearly honour. My service past, my sorrow present, and whatever merit I may yet prove—it is all yours to offer him. And if even this cannot ransom me into his love again, then at least let me know so. I'll clothe myself in contentment, however forced, and move on to whatever scraps fortune deigns to toss me."

"Alas," she replied softly, "thrice-gentle Cassio… my advocation is not now in tune. My lord is not my lord; his favour's gone, and his humour has changed with it. I would scarce know him now."

She pressed her hands together, pale knuckles standing out like carved bone.

"So help me every spirit sanctified," she continued, "I have spoken for you with all my breath, and stood full within the blank of his displeasure for my boldness. Be patient. I will do all I can—and more than I dare for myself. Let that suffice."

Just then, Iago, feigning a curiosity so perfect it might have been real, tilted his head. "Is my lord angry?"

"He went hence just now," Emilia said, "and certainly in strange unquietness."

Iago's brow creased in theatre's finest imitation of concern. "Can he be angry? I've seen him beneath cannon-fire, when the very wind of war blew the limbs from his own brother-in-arms, and he bore it with less heat than this. If he's angry—then something moves."

Desdemona nodded faintly. "I prithee, go to him."

And so Iago left, the silent poison of his absence no less potent than his speech.

Desdemona sighed and turned her gaze to the middle distance. "Something, sure, of state. From Venice, or some unhatched plot revealed here in Cyprus. It's troubled his clear spirit."

She stood and began to pace.

"In such moments," she murmured, "even great men's natures wrangle with inferior things. For what is man, if not a vessel prone to leaks? Let but our finger ache, and it clouds our whole body with pain. Nay, we must not ask of them the observances fit for bridal vows. Beshrew me—I, poor soldier of love, had arraigned him unjustly. He is not himself… and I had accused a ghost."

Emilia's eyes narrowed. "Pray heaven it be state matters, as you think, and no jealous toy. Nothing concerning you."

"Alas the day," Desdemona said, with a lift of her chin, "I never gave him cause."

Emilia paused. "But jealous souls won't be answered so. They are not jealous for the cause—they are jealous because they are jealous. 'Tis a monster born of itself, begot on its own bile."

Desdemona flinched. "Heaven keep that monster from Othello's mind."

"Lady," Emilia said with a slow, sad nod, "amen."

Desdemona turned. "I'll go seek him. Cassio, walk hereabout. If I find him fit, I'll plead your suit again."

Cassio bowed deeply. "I humbly thank your ladyship."

The two women disappeared into the palace shadows, and Cassio, left to his solitude, was not alone for long.

From the arcade there came the bright lilt of feminine irritation.

"Save you, friend Cassio!"

He turned and smiled faintly. "What make you from home? How is it with you, my most fair Bianca?"

"I'faith, sweet love, I was going to your lodging," she said, advancing in a flutter of pale muslin and reproach. "What? A week away? Seven days, seven nights? A hundred and sixty-eight hours—and each one worse than the last!"

Cassio chuckled. "Pardon me, Bianca. I have this while been pressed with heavy thoughts."

He reached into his breast and produced the fateful token—the handkerchief, Desdemona's enchanted thread of silk and omen.

"Take me this work out," he said, handing it to her as one might pass an innocent trinket. "I like it well. I would have it copied."

Bianca's eyes fell upon it, and her countenance stiffened.

"Whence came this?" she asked, her voice cooling like a shuttered hearth. "This is no work of mine. This is some token… from a newer friend."

Cassio winced. "Go to, woman! Cast your vile guesses in the devil's teeth. You are jealous now—that this is from some mistress?"

He laughed, though uneasily. "No. In good troth, Bianca."

"Why—whose is it?"

"I know not, sweet. I found it in my chamber. I like the work. And ere it be demanded—"

Bianca turned her head, still holding the handkerchief but now as if it stung her fingers. "Leave you! Wherefore?"

"I attend upon the general. 'Tis no addition to be seen in such company just now."

"Not that you love me not," she said, wounded.

"But that you do not love me," she added with a bitter smile.

Cassio reached out gently. "Walk a little with me. I must remain here, but I'll see you soon."

"It's very good," she said curtly, the silk pressed to her palm like a brand. "I must be… circumstanced."

She followed him down the veranda with a step both graceful and sullen. The curtain dropped behind them.

Inside the palace, the handkerchief's absence swirled like smoke, its threads unravelling not just silk, but fate.

ACT IV

The Dream and the Dagger

In which sleep is shattered, innocence condemned, and hell's echo finds its voice.

ACT IV SCENE 1

The morning broke, if such a word could be used for that hour in Cyprus where storm clouds swelled like the ripening belly of some foul prophecy. The air hung heavy, thick with salt and the acrid scent of cannon-cleaned iron, and the castle loomed not so much like a place of governance but a waiting tomb — each parapet silent, as if bracing itself for the whisper of swords.

Beneath this stifling canopy, before the very walls of the Venetian outpost, stood two figures — one monumental, one snake-supple — engaged in a conversation so private and so piercing that even the wind dared not intervene. Othello, General of the Venetian forces, his fine sable cloak unfastened and hanging as though from a crucifix, clenched and unclenched his gloved hand like a man praying through fury. Beside him, Iago leaned in with the posture of a man who might whisper absolution and damnation in the same breath.

"Will you think so?" Iago said lightly, the words shaped with a casualness that belied the gravity they carried.

"Think so, Iago!" Othello's voice rang out, brittle as a blade dropped on flagstone. The Moor turned, his face wrenched by disbelief.

"What?" Iago offered a small shrug. "To kiss in private?"

Othello stiffened. "An unauthorized kiss," he replied, his tongue making brittle work of the word. Iago, with a smile that seemed carved from cold meat, added softly, "Or to be naked with her friend in bed, an hour or more, not meaning any harm?"

There was a pause, and a gull screamed above — a flash of white against the brooding grey.

"Naked in bed, Iago, and not mean harm!" Othello's voice trembled with the restraint of a man standing before a noose. "That is hypocrisy against the devil himself. They claim virtue, yet do such things? Then it's the devil that tempts their virtue — and they, in turn, tempt Heaven itself."

"Still," said Iago, brushing imagined dust from his jerkin, "they've done nothing. 'Tis a venial slip. Small sin. But if I were to give my wife a handkerchief—"

"What then?" Othello snapped.

"Why then, 'tis hers, my lord. And being hers, she might bestow't on any man."

"She is protectress of her honour too," said Othello darkly. "May she give that?"

Iago smiled with false modesty, as though addressing a courtroom, not a soul on the brink. "Her honour," he mused, "is an essence that's not seen. They have it often who have it not." It was nonsense, of course — a word-game meant to madden.

"But for the handkerchief—"

"By heaven," Othello growled, "I would most gladly have forgot it."

He turned away, but the past came up like a carrion bird. "Thou said'st — it comes o'er my memory, as doth the raven o'er the infected house, boding to all..."

He stopped. His voice shrank.

"He had my handkerchief."

"Ay, what of that?" said Iago with a flick of his brow.

"That's not so good now," Othello muttered.

"What... if I had said I had seen him do you wrong?"

Othello turned, face taut, like a man staring down a musket.

"Or heard him say—" Iago continued, "as knaves be such abroad, who having supplied their lusts, whether by relentless pleading or voluntary dotage of some mistress — cannot help but blab about the act..."

"Hath he said anything?" Othello demanded.

"He hath, my lord," Iago said quietly. "But be you well assured... no more than he'll unswear." Iago had to be careful here, for he knew as well as anyone that all these accusations were conjured from the delicate air, and held together with naught but a cloth embroidered with strawberries.

"What. Hath. He. Said?"

And now Iago paused, sculpting the silence.

"'Faith," he said. "That he did— I know not what he did."

Othello's voice cracked: "What? What?"

And Iago delivered it like a death-knell: "Lie—"

"With her?"

"With her, on her — what you will."

There came a stillness, thick and eerie, as if all the air had been sucked from the scene. Othello's voice grew jagged. "Lie with her! Lie on her! We say 'lie on her' when they belie her — lie with her! That's fulsome."

His hands shook now, twitching, clenching. His eyes darted, unseeing, to some horror only he beheld. "Handkerchief... confessions... handkerchief! To confess and be hanged for his labour! First to be hanged, and then to confess— I tremble at it. Nature... would not invest herself in such shadowing passion without some instruction—" He staggered. "It is not words that shake me thus. Pish! Noses, ears, and lips — Is't possible? Confess! Handkerchief! O devil!"

He collapsed, as though struck by a cannonball. His frame convulsed once, then lay still — in the dust, like a fallen effigy. Iago, watching him with the eye of a physician-priest, whispered: "Work on, my medicine, work. Thus credulous fools are caught."

And then he straightened and cried aloud: "What, ho! My lord! My lord, I say!"

The figure who entered next might, under ordinary circumstances, have brought with him a pleasant air of recovery — a man dressed not for war but for society, with the kind of trim beard that implied both discipline and vanity. Michael Cassio — no longer lieutenant but still every inch the courtly soldier — emerged on the castle's stone walk with a studied grace. Yet behind the polish was the tension of a man walking close to power, and unsure if his next step would restore him... or ruin him.

"How now, Cassio!" Iago greeted him with a brisk, almost cheerful urgency.

Cassio blinked at the sight of Othello's body, still sprawled in the dust, his limbs twisted as though struck down by God. "What's the matter?"

"My lord," said Iago, with a voice dipped in false concern, "has fallen into an epilepsy. This is his second fit — he had one yesterday."

Cassio knelt instinctively, fumbling for the general's pulse. "Rub him about the temples—"

"No," Iago said quickly, seizing his wrist with unusual firmness. "Forbear. The lethargy must have its quiet course. If not, he foams at the mouth, and by and by breaks out to savage madness."

Cassio stared, half in alarm, half in confusion.

"Look," Iago continued. "He stirs. Do you withdraw yourself a little while — he will recover straight. When he is gone, I would speak with you upon a great occasion."

Cassio hesitated — then, with the good manners of a man taught never to contradict his social better, nodded and departed, sparing Othello a last concerned glance. He might have stayed, had he guessed the theatre in which he played the fool. Othello stirred with the slow misery of a man returning from drowning. His eyelids fluttered. His first sound was not speech but a low growl, as of some great beast rousing in the dark.

Iago crouched beside him, head tilted, eyes glinting. "How is it, general? Have you not hurt your head?"

Othello turned his face toward him, the whites of his eyes stark against the dust that streaked his cheek.

"Dost thou mock me?"

"I mock you?" Iago's voice grew sharper, touched with just enough indignation to seem sincere. "No, by heaven. Would you would bear your fortune like a man!"

Othello laughed then — a short, mirthless bark that ended in a cough. "A hornèd man's a monster and a beast," he said. His hand rose, trembling, to touch his own brow, as if he expected the cuckold's horns to have sprouted there.

"There's many a beast then," Iago replied drily, "in a populous city — and many a civil monster."

He smiled, the way a tax collector might when telling a widow her husband's debt had doubled.

Othello grunted. "Did he confess it?"

"Good sir, be a man," Iago said, almost wearily. "Think — every bearded fellow that's but yoked in marriage may be in the same boat as you. There's millions now alive that nightly lie in those unproper beds which they dare swear peculiar."

Othello looked up, slowly, his eyes narrowing.

"O, 'tis the spite of hell," said Iago with growing heat, "the fiend's arch-mock — to lip a wanton woman in a secure couch, and to suppose her chaste!"

He shook his head as if wounded by the thought. "No. Let me know — and knowing what I am, I know what she shall be."

He did not say the word — but its shadow hung in the air: whore.

Othello inhaled. The dust scraped his throat, but he did not cough. "O, thou art wise. 'Tis certain."

Here, at last, came surrender.

A strange silence settled — as though all the sound in the world had gone somewhere else. Even the gulls, overhead, were mute.

Iago stepped back a pace. "Stand you awhile apart," he said. "Confine yourself in a patient list." His tone shifted, softening as one might when instructing a madman to sit quietly with his own ghosts. "Whilst you were here overwhelmed with your grief — a passion most unsuiting such a man — Cassio came hither."

Othello's brow twitched.

"I shifted him away," Iago went on. "Laid good excuse upon your ecstasy. Bade him return, and here speak with me — which he promised."

He stepped closer, now pressing words into Othello's ear as if they were poison through a straw.

"Do but encave yourself," he said. "And mark the fleers, the gibes, the notable scorns that dwell in every region of his face."

Here Iago's voice became theatrical, almost amused.

"For I will make him tell the tale anew — where, how, how oft, how long ago, and when he hath — and is again — to cope your wife." The word squirmed with euphemism. Othello's mouth twitched.

"I say," Iago finished, "but mark his gesture. Marry, patience — or I shall say you are all in all in spleen, and nothing of a man."

He stepped back, leaving Othello to seethe alone.

Thus ended the second act of Iago's trap, and the Moor, like a man who sees an assassin coming and thinks him some long-lost acquaintance, took his place behind the curtain, to watch — to witness — to burn.

Othello, still panting from his convulsion, had retreated behind a heavy column, its chipped stone bearing the gouges of old siegework. There he crouched, half-shadowed, his fingers digging into his knees as he listened.

"Dost thou hear, Iago?" he whispered hoarsely. "I will be found most cunning in my patience." His jaw clenched, his teeth audible like a lock snapping shut. "But — dost thou hear? — most bloody."

Iago bowed his head as though to a sovereign. "That's not amiss," he murmured. "But yet — keep time in all. Will you withdraw?"

And so the Moor withdrew, folding himself into silence with the intensity of a starving man who dares not yet reach for the feast.

Now alone, Iago turned to the trap's final spring.

Now will I question Cassio of Bianca, he thought to himself, his smile sharp as shears. Bianca was a 'housewife' that, by selling her desires, bought herself bread and clothes. A poor creature that doted on Cassio; as is the strumpet's plague to beguile many, and be beguiled by one. He chuckled. "He, when he hears of her, cannot refrain from the excess of laughter."

And lo — as if summoned by the devil's own cue — Cassio entered.

"Lieutenant," Iago greeted. "How do you now?"

Cassio winced slightly. "The worser," he said, "that you give me the addition whose want even kills me." A subtle complaint — the pain of demotion, the ache of a reputation unstitched.

"Ply Desdemona well," said Iago, voice loud. "And you are sure on't."

Then, a short whisper in the man's ear — with a wink sharp enough to cut a peach — "Now, if this suit lay in Bianca's power, how quickly should you speed!"

Cassio laughed, that golden soldier's laugh. "Alas, poor caitiff!"

Behind the column, Othello stirred. Iago had disguised the change in conversation to Bianca. Othello believed them still to be on the topic of his fair wife.

"Look how he laughs already!" he hissed through clenched teeth.

"I never knew woman love man so," Iago remarked with an artful sigh.

"Alas, poor rogue!" Cassio grinned. "I think, i'faith, she loves me."

Now Othello's mind twisted like burning parchment. He laughs — and confesses. Lies and laughs. And loves?

"Now he denies it faintly," Othello muttered to himself. "And laughs it out — laughs it out!"

Iago leaned forward. "Do you hear, Cassio?"

Othello, rapt. "Now he importunes him... to tell it o'er. Go to — well said, well said."

"She gives it out," Iago said, "that you shall marry her. Do you intend it?"

Cassio exploded with laughter. "Ha, ha, ha!"

Behind the stone, Othello's breath caught.

"Do you triumph, Roman?" he murmured. "Do you triumph?"

Cassio, oblivious to the gory theatre his voice now starred in, waved a hand. "I marry her? What — a customer?" He raised both eyebrows in mock horror. "Prithee, bear some charity to my wit — do not think it so unwholesome! Ha, ha, ha!"

Othello's voice dropped to a deadly whisper. "So. So, so, so. They laugh that win."

"'Faith," said Iago, as if driving the nail home with a sigh, "the cry goes that you shall marry her."

"Prithee, say true."

"I am a very villain else," Iago said with great theatrical solemnity.

Othello, watching from behind the column, nodded slowly — as a judge might after hearing damning testimony.

"Have you scored me?" he whispered. "Well."

Cassio, ever the jester, shrugged. "This is the monkey's own giving out. She is persuaded I will marry her, out of her own love and flattery — not out of my promise."

Othello leaned forward. "Iago beckons me... now he begins the story."

He pressed himself tighter to the stone, body taut, mind ablaze. The trap had been baited with Bianca — but Othello, watching with the eyes of a madman, saw Desdemona in her stead. Every grin became an admission; every word, a dagger.

And so, with laughter still ringing through the Cyprus air, the final knots of Iago's noose were drawn tight.

"She was here even now," said Cassio, brushing dust from his sleeve. "She haunts me in every place."

Othello, behind the stone, leaned closer.

"I was the other day talking on the sea-bank with certain Venetians," Cassio continued with a chuckle, "and thither comes the bauble — and by this hand, she falls me thus about my neck—"

Othello mouthed the words in tandem: "Crying 'O dear Cassio!' as it were: his gesture imports it."

Cassio, laughing, pantomimed a woman's clinging: arms flung about the neck, head buried in the shoulder, shoulders shaking with exaggerated sobs.

"So hangs, and lolls, and weeps upon me," he said merrily, "so hales, and pulls me — ha, ha, ha!"

Othello's vision swam. He saw Desdemona's face where Bianca's should have been — her arms, her tears, her voice crying Cassio. The laughter rang out like a bell at a funeral.

"Now he tells how she plucked him to my chamber," Othello muttered. "O, I see that nose of yours... but not that dog I shall throw it to."

Cassio clapped his hands together lightly. "Well — I must leave her company."

Iago, alert to his cue, turned and gestured. "Before me! Look, where she comes."

Cassio rolled his eyes. "'Tis such another fitchew, same as any other polecat, except this one wears perfume."

And so entered Bianca, in all her tempestuous glory. A woman of considerable presence, with hair piled high and eyes that snapped with fury. Her gown was of questionable modesty and unapologetic expense, dyed a deep crimson that seemed to shout her mood before she spoke. The scent of musk and orange blossom preceded her like a storm warning.

"What do you mean by this haunting of me?" Cassio asked, hands raised as though to ward her off.

Bianca's voice was a flung goblet. "Let the devil and his dam haunt you!" she cried. "What did you mean by that same handkerchief you gave me even now?"

Othello surged forward slightly.

"I was a fine fool to take it," she went on, each syllable sharpened on a whetstone of rage. "I must take out the stitching work? A likely piece of work, that you should find it in your chamber — and not know who left it there!"

Othello froze. His breath came in shallow stabs. The handkerchief.

"This is some minx's token," Bianca spat. "And I must take out the work? There! Give it back to your hobby-horse — wheresoever you had it, I'll take out no work on't."

She flung the embroidered cloth at Cassio, who caught it with the surprised grace of a man who had dropped a coin and received a curse.

"How now, my sweet Bianca?" Cassio said, suddenly all silk and flattery. "How now! How now!"

But Othello had eyes only for the fluttering fabric in her hand. His voice, low and stunned, emerged from the shadows:

"By heaven, that should be my handkerchief."

Bianca turned on her heel. "An you'll come to supper to-night, you may. An you will not — come when you are next prepared for."

She swept away like a frigate under full sail, crimson skirts billowing, perfume and fury trailing in her wake.

"After her," Iago whispered. "After her."

Cassio groaned. "'Faith, I must — she'll rail in the street else."

"Will you sup there?"

"'Faith, I intend so."

"Well, I may chance to see you," Iago said lightly, "for I would very fain speak with you."

"Prithee, come. Will you?"

"Go to. Say no more."

Cassio vanished into the labyrinth of stone, his whistle echoing lightly behind him.

Then silence fell — the kind that feels loud in the soul. Othello stepped forward.

"Did you perceive how he laughed at his vice?" Iago asked, still watching the space where Cassio had gone.

Othello's voice cracked. "O Iago!"

"And did you see the handkerchief?"

"Was that mine?"

"Yours, by this hand," said Iago. "And to see how he prizes the foolish woman — your wife! She gave it him. And he hath given it his whore."

A silence. Then Othello, almost to himself: "I would have him nine years a-killing."

His eyes welled — but no tears fell. Only rage.

"A fine woman!" he cried suddenly. "A fair woman! A sweet woman!"

Iago's voice was cold. "Nay. You must forget that."

"Ay," Othello muttered, "let her rot, and perish, and be damned to-night. For she shall not live. No — my heart is turned to stone; I strike it, and it hurts my hand."

He clenched his fist, trembling.

"O, the world hath not a sweeter creature. She might lie by an emperor's side — and command him tasks."

"That's not your way," said Iago.

"Hang her!" Othello roared. "I do but say what she is. So delicate with her needle — an admirable musician! She will sing the savageness out of a bear — of so high and plenteous wit and invention—"

"She's the worse for all this," Iago said quietly.

Othello groaned. "O — a thousand thousand times. And then — of so gentle a condition!"

Iago, softly: "Ay. Too gentle."

And in the hush that followed, Othello's love became a weapon, and his sorrow curdled into murder. Othello, eyes glassed with conviction, turned once more to Iago. His voice was quieter now — like a butcher consulting his ledger.

"Nay, that's certain," he said, as if ticking off a price. "But yet — the pity of it, Iago!"

He paused, his face convulsing with a terrible ache.

"O Iago... the pity of it, Iago!"

And for a breath, he was a man again — a husband clutching the ghost of what he once believed. But Iago, who suffered no ghosts, offered only iron. "If you are so fond over her iniquity, give her patent to offend, nay encourage her. For if it bothers not you — it bothers nobody."

Othello's fist tightened.

"I will chop her into messes! Cuckold me!"

"'Tis foul in her," Iago replied with solemn nod.

"With mine officer!" Othello snarled.

"That's fouler."

"Get me some poison, Iago — this night. I'll not expostulate with her, lest her body and beauty unprovide my mind again. This night, Iago."

Iago's eyes gleamed with clinical pleasure. "Do it not with poison. Strangle her in her bed. Even the bed she hath contaminated."

Othello's face lit like a martyr's pyre.

"Good. Good. The justice of it pleases — very good."

But just then, from within the castle, came the shrill blast of a trumpet.

"What trumpet is that same?" Othello barked.

Iago craned his neck toward the gate. "Something from Venice, sure. 'Tis Lodovico — come from the Duke. And see, your wife is with him."

The company entered like figures in a tableau — Lodovico bearing and official letter, a man of grave bearing and calm manners; Desdemona walking beside him, angelic in white, her face as open as prayer; and behind them, attendants in the livery of Venetian state.

"Save you, worthy general!" said Lodovico.

"With all my heart, sir," Othello replied, bowing stiffly.

"The Duke and senators of Venice greet you." Lodovico extended a letter.

"I kiss the instrument of their pleasures," Othello said, and broke the seal with a ceremonial grace. His brow furrowed as he read.

Desdemona, ever the gentle hostess, turned to her kinsman. "What's the news, good cousin Lodovico?"

"I am very glad to see you, signior," said Iago, bowing low. "Welcome to Cyprus."

"I thank you. How does Lieutenant Cassio?"

"Lives, sir," said Iago.

Desdemona interjected gently: "Cousin, there's fall'n between him and my lord an unkind breach — but you shall make all well."

"Are you sure of that?" Othello asked without looking up.

Desdemona blinked. "My lord?"

Othello's eyes stayed fixed on the parchment. He read part of it out loud "'That fail you not to do, as you will—'"

Lodovico leaned toward her. "He did not call. He's busy in the paper. Is there division 'twixt my lord and Cassio?"

"A most unhappy one," said Desdemona, sweetly. "I would do much to atone them — for the love I bear to Cassio."

And with that, the powder keg exploded.

"Fire and brimstone!" Othello roared, flinging the letter to the floor.

"My lord?" Desdemona gasped.

"Are you wise?" he barked, his voice cracking.

"What — is he angry?" she turned to Lodovico, confused.

"May be the letter moved him," said Lodovico uncertainly. "For, as I think, they do command him home — deputing Cassio in his government."

"Trust me, I am glad on't," said Desdemona, smiling through her concern.

"Indeed!" Othello echoed, his voice dark as a thundercloud.

"My lord?"

"I am glad to see you mad. You can scarcely contain yourself…"

"Why, sweet Othello—" Desdemona, puzzled and trembling, took a small step toward her love — as though closeness might soften him, as though kindness might still work.

He struck her.

Her forward step became a vector, his hand the counterforce. Their motions collided like clockwork violence — a pendulum, a wrecking ball. The sound rang through the hall like a gavel dropped in shock. Desdemona recoiled, one hand to her cheek, the other raised not in defence but disbelief.

"I have not deserved this," she whispered.

"My lord," said Lodovico, aghast, "this would not be believed in Venice, though I should swear I saw't. 'Tis very much. Make her amends. She weeps."

"O devil, devil!" Othello spat. "If that the earth could teem with woman's tears, each drop she falls would prove a crocodile."

He turned on her like a blade. "Out of my sight!"

"I will not stay to offend you." She turned to go, a shimmer of salt trembling in her lashes.

"Truly," Lodovico murmured, "an obedient lady. I do beseech your lordship — call her back."

"Mistress!" cried Othello, sarcasm dripping like her tears.

"My lord?" she wasn't sure if he meant her, to be addressed such was hurtful, but she was already stunned from the slap.

"What would you with her, sir?" Othello snapped.

"Who, I, my lord?" Lodovico was almost as stunned as poor Desdemona.

"Ay — you did wish that I would make her turn. Sir, she can turn — and turn — and yet go on — and turn again! And she can weep, sir, weep!"

He stared at her.

"And she's obedient, as you say — obedient. Very obedient. Proceed you in your tears. Concerning this, sir — O well-painted passion!" His imagery of turning and painted passions sounded more lewd than any of Iago's inuendos. The entire room stood in shame and indignity, disbelief at the dramatic tragedy playing before their eyes. "I am commanded home. Get you away. I'll send for you anon." Desdemona paused — but Othello's gesture was final.

"Sir," he said to Lodovico, "I obey the mandate. And will return to Venice. Hence. Avaunt."

She departed. Only the faint sound of her slippers remained, ghostlike on the stone.

"Cassio shall have my place," Othello said. "And, sir — tonight, I do entreat that we may sup together. You are welcome, sir, to Cyprus." Again, his sarcastic tone was caustic to the bone.

He turned away and, as his heavy footsteps reverberated off the black and white tiles of the chamber, he shouted "Goats and monkeys!"

And he was gone, even as his words echoed around the nobles assembled on the checkboard of silence. Lodovico remained, stunned.

"Is this the noble Moor whom our full Senate call 'all in all sufficient'? Is this the nature whom passion could not shake?"

Iago offered a sigh so soft it might have been mistaken for sympathy.

"He is much changed."

"Are his wits safe? Is he not light of brain?" It sounded like a jest, but Lodovico was serious.

"He's that he is," said Iago. "I may not breathe my censure — what he might be. If what he might he is not, I would to heaven he were!"

Lodovico shook his head. "What — strike his wife!?"

"'Faith, that was not so well," Iago admitted. "Yet — would I knew that stroke would prove the worst."

"Is he always thus?" Lodovico asked bitterly. "Or did the letters work upon his blood, and new-create this fault?"

Iago looked to the far corridor, where Desdemona's sobs had long since faded. "Alas. Alas. It is not honesty in me to speak what I have seen and known."

He turned to Lodovico, face solemn. "You shall observe him. And his own courses will denote him so that I may save my speech. Do but go after — and mark how he continues."

"I am sorry," said Lodovico quietly, "that I am deceived in him."

And so they departed, one after the other — a nobleman in shame, and a villain in perfect composure — leaving behind only silence and echoes.

ACT IV SCENE 2

The room was narrow, plain, and lit only by the long sigh of afternoon light that spilled across the floor like the blade of a sword. A breeze stirred the gauze curtains, but could not freshen the air, which seemed thick with judgment — as though justice, or its perversion, had grown scent. Emilia stood upright, arms folded, lips firm. She had been summoned not as servant but as witness — and she bore herself accordingly.

"You have seen nothing, then?" Othello's voice was low and clipped, like a blade tapped lightly against a whetstone.

"Nor ever heard," Emilia replied, "nor ever did suspect."

"Yes," Othello countered. "You have seen Cassio and she together."

Emilia's brow furrowed, but her gaze did not flinch. "But then I saw no harm — and then I heard each syllable that breath made up between them."

Othello turned from her and stared at the wall, as though words alone were insufficient proof of guilt, but he might find it in the plaster cracks.

"What, did they never whisper?"

"Never, my lord."

"Nor send you out o' the way?"

"Never."

"To fetch her fan? Her gloves? Her mask — nor nothing?"

"Never, my lord," Emilia said again, her voice now sharpened with indignation.

Othello was silent for a moment. He turned, his eyes dark, and muttered: "That's strange."

Emilia took one step forward. "I dare, my lord — to wager she is honest — lay down my soul at stake. If you think otherwise, remove your thought — it doth abuse your bosom."

She clasped her hands, her whole frame alive with a righteous, maternal wrath. "If any wretch have put this in your head, let Heaven requite it with the serpent's curse!"

She pointed, not to Othello, but to the very air — as if daring the devil himself to manifest.

"For if she be not honest, chaste, and true," Emilia said, with terrible finality, "then there's no man happy — the purest of their wives is foul as slander."

Othello, unmoved, gestured. "Bid her come hither. Go."

Emilia hesitated a beat, then turned and left, skirts rustling like distant thunderclouds.

Left alone, Othello stared at the floor as if it might yield some different verdict. "She says enough," he muttered. "Yet she's a simple bawd that cannot say as much. This is a subtle whore, a closet lock and key of villainous secrets. And yet she'll kneel and pray — I have seen her do't."

The door creaked. Desdemona entered. Her steps were quiet, her eyes searching. Behind her, Emilia lingered only a moment, then bowed and retreated. The door closed like a tombstone falling shut.

"My lord, what is your will?" Desdemona asked gently.

"Pray, chuck — come hither."

There was something strange in his voice — too tender, and yet not kind. She stepped forward cautiously.

"What is your pleasure?"

"Let me see your eyes." He came close. "Look in my face."

She did. She looked into his eyes, as he asked.

And something looked back.

Not the man who once wooed her with his stories, nor the lover who touched her hand like it was parchment blessed by saints. No — this was the soldier, the general, the veteran of twenty campaigns. The man who could watch cities burn. The man who knew what it meant to end life after life in the service of something he believed.

In his penetrating gaze, she saw both the rage and the discipline — cold, focused, terrifying in its clarity. The gaze of a man who might do anything if he believed it righteous. She felt her breath catch, her limbs fail her just slightly. Something in her broke, like the quiet of a door closing. It was the death of her naivety. The sudden, female knowledge — ancient, unspoken — that while men may fear being mocked by love, women fear they may be murdered by it. And suddenly she knew where she was, she had been there all her life. She was trapped in one of those blank white spaces at the edge of the world, where women wait to be spoken for, or spoken against.

"What horrible fancy's this?" she whispered.

He turned To Emilia, barking toward the door, "Leave procreants alone and shut the door. Cough, or cry 'hem' if anybody come. Your job, your station — nay, dispatch."

Emilia, scandalised and confused, departed in silence. Desdemona turned back, more solemn now. "Upon my knees — what doth your speech import? I understand a fury in your words — but not the words."

Othello stepped forward, the light glancing from his brow like steel.

"Why, what art thou?"

"Your wife, my lord. Your true and loyal wife."

He came closer. "Come, swear it. Damn thyself — lest, being like one of heaven, the devils themselves should fear to seize thee. Therefore be double-damned. Swear thou art honest!"

Desdemona faltered. "Heaven doth truly know it."

Othello's voice was now as low and cold as water in a grave. "Heaven truly knows that thou art false as hell."

"To whom, my lord?" she cried. "With whom? How am I false?"

But he turned from her — like a man unwilling to look upon his own executioner. "O Desdemona! Away! Away! Away!"

"Alas, the heavy day!" Desdemona fell back as if struck by light alone. "Why do you weep? Am I the motive of these tears, my lord?"

She stepped forward, voice trembling.

"If haply you my father do suspect — an instrument of this your calling back — lay not your blame on me. If you have lost him, why, I have lost him too."

Othello stood motionless. Like a statue carved in rage.

There came a pause — not silence, for Othello's breath was ragged, and Desdemona's skirt whispered faintly as she knelt — but a moment where the very air shuddered, as though the walls had caught wind of what was to follow and recoiled from it.

"Had it pleased heaven," Othello said at last, his voice hollow and majestic, "to try me with affliction—"

He lifted his arms slightly, palms upward, like a priest upon a desecrated altar.

"Had they rain'd all kinds of sores and shames upon my bare head, steep'd me in poverty to the very lips, given to captivity me and my utmost hopes..."

Desdemona dared not speak. She watched him now as a girl might watch a wild animal pace its cage — the beauty of him made more terrible by the thought of sudden violence.

"I should have found in some place of my soul a drop of patience," he said, his tone trembling at the edge of a sob.

He turned away from her, toward the casement window, though he saw no sky.

"But alas — to make me a fixed figure for the time of scorn to point his slow, unmoving finger at! Yet — could I bear that too. Well. Very well."

His voice dropped. His brow folded like paper being crushed.

"But there — where I have garner'd up my heart, where either I must live, or bear no life — the fountain from which my current runs, or else dries up — to be discarded thence!"

He turned to her now, eyes ablaze.

"Or keep it as a cistern for foul toads to knot and gender in!"

He reached for the heavens with one trembling hand.

"Turn thy complexion there, Patience! Thou young and rose-lipp'd cherubin — ay, there, look grim as hell!"

It was the cry of a man betrayed not just by his wife, but by his own capacity to love.

Desdemona could not help but speak. "I hope my noble lord esteems me honest."

He wheeled upon her.

"O, ay — as summer flies are in the shambles — that quicken even with blowing! Flies in the meat market, sweetness rooted in filth. O thou weed!"

The words struck her like stones.

"Who art so lovely fair, and smell'st so sweet, that the sense aches at thee — would thou hadst ne'er been born!"

Desdemona's voice cracked. "Alas — what ignorant sin have I committed?"

Othello approached now, slow and dreadful.

"Was this fair paper, this most goodly book — made to write 'whore' upon?"

He took her chin, lifted it — his touch as cold as verdict.

"What committed?" he barked. "Committed! O thou public commoner! I should make very forges of my cheeks, that would to cinders burn up modesty, did I but speak thy deeds."

She flinched — but did not fall.

"What committed!" he roared. "Heaven stops the nose at it, and the moon winks! The bawdy wind that kisses all it meets is hush'd within the hollow mine of earth and will not hear it. What committed! Impudent strumpet!"

Desdemona backed away, pale as frost. "By heaven — you do me wrong!"

"Are you not a strumpet?"

"No — as I am a Christian! If to preserve this vessel for my lord from any other foul, unlawful touch be not to be a strumpet — I am none!"

Othello paused, his expression briefly unreadable.

"What — not a whore?"

"No. As I shall be saved."

There came a beat of absolute stillness. Then Othello whispered, as though to some phantom seated beside him:

"Is't possible?"

Desdemona closed her eyes. "O heaven forgive us."

And in that moment, perhaps — just perhaps — his doubt returned. A crack in the stone.

"I cry you mercy, then," he said faintly. "I took you for that cunning whore of Venice that married with Othello."

He raised his voice now — loud, public, theatrical:

"You, mistress! That have the office opposite to Saint Peter, and keep the gate of hell!"

The door opened, and Emilia re-entered as one might enter a sickroom, wary yet urgent.

"You! You, ay, you!" Othello barked. "We have done our course — there's money for your pains. I pray you — turn the key and keep our counsel."

He thrust a few coins into her hand — aping the conclusive transaction at a brothel, a cold gratuity for services rendered. And with that, he turned and left, his cloak sweeping behind him like smoke in a burning room. Emilia looked after him, then to Desdemona, who stood trembling, a woman now, shattered, but still upright.

"Alas," she said, her eyes flitting from the closing door to her mistress's face, "what does this gentleman conceive?"

Desdemona turned toward her slowly, her face pale with confusion more than pain — like a saint newly told that heaven had been revoked.

"How do you, madam? How do you, my good lady?"

"'Faith," Desdemona murmured, "half asleep."

Her voice held that odd clarity which sometimes attends despair — the calm of a body going under.

"Good madam, what's the matter with my lord?"

Desdemona blinked. "With who?"

Emilia frowned. "Why — with my lord, madam."

There was a silence, and then — with infinite gentleness — Desdemona replied:

"Who is thy lord?"

Emilia stared.

"He that is yours, sweet lady."

Desdemona shook her head with a strange, faint smile. "I have none. Do not talk to me, Emilia. I cannot weep. Nor answer have I none, but tears."

She looked up, her eyes shining but dry. "Prithee — tonight, lay on my bed my wedding sheets. Remember."

She turned away, then added softly, "And call thy husband hither."

Emilia paused — struck by the poignancy of the request. Though odd to modern ears, it rang with quiet ritual and custom. In certain corners of Christendom — and nowhere with more ceremony than in Venice — a bride's honour was not merely a moral abstraction, but a thing to be witnessed, certified, and, in some families of considerable fuss, displayed. The bedlinen of the bridal night, if it bore the red mark of virginity, could become a kind of domestic relic — evidence of chastity rendered in cotton and consequence. On rare occasions it was paraded with as much pomp as a new coat-of-arms. On others, merely inspected and folded away, like a receipt for a transaction completed in flesh. That Desdemona should request those very sheets now — on a night shadowed by suspicion, slander, and something colder still — was no accident. If she could not speak her innocence, perhaps she might lie in it, visibly, quietly, and surrounded by the last proof her husband had ever trusted. Emilia understood, had always understood. Such customs were scripted for women to perform, but they were shaped by male fear, stylised by the male gaze. Emilia simply curtsied and departed, her footsteps tapping like the slow drip of water in a forgotten well.

Desdemona, now alone again, whispered to herself:

"'Tis meet I should be used so. Very meet."

She crossed the room to the long, narrow window. A single dove sat on the sill, indifferent to human tragedy.

"How have I been behaved," she asked the bird, or the wind, "that he might stick the small'st opinion on my least misuse?"

The light in the room began to diminish, Desdemona was barely aware of the time passing, her thoughts flew away like the dove she was speaking to. Then the door opened again, and Emilia returned — Iago at her side, looking composed, inquisitive, feigning concern with the mastery that was the mystery of his craft.

"What is your pleasure, madam?" he asked smoothly. "How is't with you?"

Desdemona did not answer at once. Her voice, when it came, was distant and sad.

"I cannot tell. Those that do teach young babes do it with gentle means and easy tasks. He might have chid me so; for, in good faith, I am a child to chiding."

Iago frowned — a mask of pity.

"What's the matter, lady?"

Emilia answered for her.

"Alas, Iago — my lord hath so bewhored her. Thrown such despite and heavy terms upon her, as true hearts cannot bear."

Desdemona looked up. "Am I that name, Iago?"

"What name, fair lady?"

"Such as she says my lord did say I was."

Emilia stepped forward, eyes blazing. "He call'd her whore! A beggar in his drink could not have laid such terms upon his callet!"

"Why did he so?" Iago asked — too quickly.

"I do not know," Desdemona whispered. "I am sure I am none such."

"Do not weep," said Iago. "Do not weep. Alas the day!"

But Emilia was no longer quiet. Her voice rose, gaining heat and shape like iron in a smith's fire.

"Hath she forsook so many noble matches — her father, her country, and her friends — to be call'd whore? Would it not make one weep?"

Desdemona bowed her head. "It is my wretched fortune."

"Beshrew him for't!" cried Iago. "How comes this trick upon him?"

"Nay," said Desdemona gently. "Heaven doth know."

But Emilia would not let it lie.

"I will be hang'd," she declared, "if some eternal villain — some busy and insinuating rogue, some cogging, cozening slave to get some office — hath not devised this slander! I'll be hang'd else."

Iago stiffened.

"Fie, there is no such man," he said lightly. "It is impossible."

Desdemona nodded faintly. "If any such there be, heaven pardon him."

But Emilia spat the word. "A noose pardon him! And hell gnaw his bones! Why should he call her whore? Who keeps her company? What place? What time? What form? What likelihood?"

Her voice had grown thunderous now, rich with righteous fire.

"The Moor's abused by some most villainous knave — some base, notorious knave — some scurvy fellow!"

She turned to the ceiling, as though addressing Heaven's very architects.

"O heaven! That such companions thou'ldst unfold — and put in every honest hand a whip to lash the rascals naked through the world, even from the east to the west!"

"Speak within door!" snapped Iago, his temper flaring for just a breath.

But Emilia was not cowed.

"O, fie upon them! Some such squire he was that turn'd your wit the seamy side without — and made you to suspect me with the Moor!"

"You are a fool," Iago snarled. "Go to."

And with that, he turned sharply, leaving Emilia mid-breath and Desdemona on the cusp of tears. Desdemona, still kneeling, turned to Iago like a pilgrim turns to a shrine — not with faith, but with the frail hope that something sacred might still dwell there.

"O good Iago," she said softly, "what shall I do to win my lord again?"

Her voice, tender and broken, might have melted stone — but it struck only the waxy polish of Iago's concern.

"Good friend," she pleaded, "go to him. For by this light of heaven, I know not how I lost him."

She lowered herself further, her hands clasped in pure entreaty.

"Here I kneel: if e'er my will did trespass 'gainst his love, either in discourse of thought or actual deed — or that mine eyes, mine ears, or any sense delighted them in any other form…"

Her throat trembled.

"Or that I do not yet, and ever did — and ever will — though he do shake me off to beggarly divorcement — love him dearly…"

She drew in a breath, voice faltering.

"Comfort forswear me! Unkindness may do much — and his unkindness may defeat my life, but never taint my love."

Then came the line, so tragic in its innocence, that the air itself recoiled:

"I cannot say 'whore' — it does abhor me now I speak the word. To do the act that might the addition earn — not the world's mass of vanity could make me."

Iago, whose heart was all mechanism, clicked gently into response.

"I pray you," he said, "be content. 'Tis but his humour — the business of the state does him offence, and he does chide with you."

Desdemona looked at him long. "If 'twere no other..."

"'Tis but so, I warrant."

Just then, trumpets sounded from within. The summons to supper, the return of the formal world — a world Desdemona no longer belonged to.

"Hark," Iago said. "How these instruments summon to supper! The messengers of Venice stay the meat. Go in, and weep not. All things shall be well."

She nodded, rising like a ghost. Emilia followed. Together they departed, one weeping, one watching.

The room was empty for a beat. Then Roderigo slinked into the room. His boots were dusty, his beard patchier than pride would allow, and his expression that of a man whose idiocy had begun to itch.

"How now, Roderigo," Iago called cheerily, like a bartender greeting a debtor.

"I do not find," said Roderigo, "that thou dealest justly with me."

Iago raised his brows. "What in the contrary?"

"Every day thou daffest me with some device, Iago!" Roderigo snapped. "And rather — as it seems to me now — keepest from me all conveniency than suppliest me with the least advantage of hope."

He thumped his chest, a pitiful display of bravado.

"I will no longer endure it. Nor am I yet persuaded to put up in peace what I have foolishly suffered."

Iago raised a calming hand. "Will you hear me, Roderigo?"

"'Faith, I've heard too much! For your words and performances are no kin together."

"You charge me most unjustly."

"With nought but truth!" Roderigo barked. "I have wasted myself out of my means! The jewels you had from me to deliver to Desdemona would half have corrupted a votarist! And what have I in return? Nothing."

Iago sighed. "Well. Go to. Very well."

"Very well? Go to?" Roderigo stamped his foot. "'Tis not very well! I think it is scurvy! I begin to find myself fobbed in it!"

"Very well," Iago repeated, now positively funereal in tone.

"I tell you, it is not very well," Roderigo growled. "I will make myself known to Desdemona. If she return me my jewels, I will give over my suit and repent my unlawful solicitation. If not — assure yourself I will seek satisfaction of you." He tried to peel off a glove — the classic challenge — but his hands were sweating, and the damn thing wouldn't budge. He abandoned it, jaw tight. The threat had been issued, if not quite performed.

"You have said now," Iago said, almost admiringly.

"Ay — and said nothing but what I intend doing."

Now Iago brightened.

"Why — now I see there's mettle in thee. And even from this instant, I build on thee a better opinion than ever before."

He clasped Roderigo's loose-gloved hand, warm and false.

"Thou hast taken against me a most just exception — but yet, I protest, I have dealt most directly in thy affair."

Roderigo frowned. "It hath not appeared."

"I grant indeed it hath not appeared," Iago replied, "and your suspicion is not without wit and judgment."

Then his voice dropped, soft and conspiratorial:

"But, Roderigo — if thou hast that in thee indeed, which I have greater reason to believe now than ever — I mean purpose, courage, and valour — this night show it."

He stepped closer. "If thou the next night following enjoy not Desdemona, take me from this world with treachery, and devise engines for my life."

"Well," said Roderigo, voice lowering. "What is it? Is it within reason and compass?"

"Ay," said Iago. "There is especial commission come from Venice to depute Cassio in Othello's place."

"Is that true?" Roderigo stiffened. "Then Othello and Desdemona return to Venice?"

"O, no." Iago shook his head. "He goes into Mauritania — and takes with him the fair Desdemona, unless his abode be lingered here by some accident — wherein none can be so determinate as the removing of Cassio."

Roderigo blinked. "How do you mean — removing of him?"

Iago spoke the next line with brutal calm: "Why — by making him uncapable of Othello's place. Knocking out his brains."

"And you would have me do it?"

"Ay — if you dare do yourself a profit and a right. He sups tonight with a harlotry, and thither will I go to him. He knows not yet of his horrorable fortune."

He turned, beckoning.

"If you will watch his going thence — which I will fashion to fall out between twelve and one — you may take him at your pleasure. I will be near to second your attempt, and he shall fall between us."

He clapped Roderigo on the back.

"Come — stand not amazed at it, but go along with me. I will show you such a necessity in his death that you shall think yourself bound to put it on him."

He stepped back, arms wide.

"It is now high suppertime — and the night grows to waste. About it."

Roderigo, bewildered but beguiled, nodded. "I will hear further reason for this."

"And you," said Iago with a smile, "shall be satisfied."

They exited, one led by desperation, the other by design — and the castle's halls fell once more into shadow, echoing with laughter that had never been sincere.

ACT IV SCENE 3

The antechamber was still and candlelit, a private room tucked away in the deeper recesses of the castle — neither grand nor lowly, but charged with the quiet tension of a space long haunted by female sorrow. The walls held their breath. The hearth, though stoked, gave off no warmth.

Desdemona stood by the casement, her fingers laced before her, her figure upright yet strange — like a statue just learning to move. Behind her, Emilia lingered, hands full of silks and pins, eyes darting with fretful affection.

From the adjoining room came the sound of voices concluding the last turns of business — murmurs, formalities, the close of a judgment. Then: boots. High-ranking ones, well-heeled and burdened by secrets.

Othello entered the antechamber, followed by Lodovico and a small group of attendants.

"I do beseech you, sir," said the Venetian lord, "trouble yourself no further."

Othello's voice was calm, unusually so.

"O, pardon me," he replied. "'Twill do me good to walk."

Lodovico turned to Desdemona and offered a parting gesture of courtly gratitude.

"Madam, good night; I humbly thank your ladyship."

"Your honour is most welcome," she said with perfect poise, though her hands were curled tightly in her skirts.

Othello paused in the doorway, casting a glance that carried none of the warmth a husband might offer his wife at bedtime. His next words were coldly practical.

"Will you walk, sir?" he asked Lodovico.

And then — a beat too late to be casual:

"O — Desdemona —"

She looked up quickly, still hoping for some note of tenderness in his voice.

"My lord?"

"Get you to bed on the instant," he said. "I will be returned forthwith. Dismiss your attendant there. Look it be done."

There was no warmth in the command, only finality. Desdemona bowed her head and said nothing more. The men departed like magistrates leaving a courtroom, the sentence unspoken but understood.

Othello's voice lingered in the air still, as though it had stained the walls.

"I will," Desdemona murmured, repeating the last command her husband had given her. She did not speak with bitterness, but with something quieter, something that had begun to look like acceptance.

Emilia approached softly. "How goes it now? He looked gentler than he did."

Desdemona turned slightly, a ghost of a smile flickering on her lips. "He says he will return shortly. He hath commanded me to go to bed… and bade me to dismiss you."

"Dismiss me?" Emilia asked, affronted.

"It was his bidding," Desdemona said simply. "Therefore, good Emilia… give me my nightly wearing, and adieu. We must not now displease him."

At this Emilia's hands faltered, and she gave a soft, bitter laugh.

"I would you had never seen him."

Desdemona looked up, calm and earnest. "So would not I. My love doth so approve him, that even his stubbornness, his cheques, his frowns—"

She sat, and gestured for the lacing to begin.

"Prithee, unpin me — have grace and favour in them."

Emilia began her task, though her fingers trembled. "I have laid those sheets you bade me on the bed." Emilia had already seen the blood there after the first night, though had it been white as snow she would not have any cause to doubt her lady's chastity. Not all women bleed the same, she knew.

"All's one," Desdemona said dreamily. "Good faith, how foolish are our minds!"

And then, almost as an aside — yet heavy as a bell toll:

"If I do die before thee, prithee… shroud me in one of those same sheets."

Emilia froze.

"Come, come," she said gently. "You talk."

But Desdemona shook her head. "My mother had a maid called Barbara. She was in love, and he she loved proved mad… and did forsake her."

She stood now, half-laced, her voice dropping into rhythm.

"She had a song of willow," she said. "An old thing, 'twas… but it expressed her fortune. And she died… singing it."

She turned to Emilia, her eyes far off.

"That song tonight will not go from my mind. I have much to do — but to go hang my head all at one side, and sing it… like poor Barbara."

She sat again, whispering, "Prithee, dispatch."

"Shall I go fetch your night-gown?"

"No — unpin me here." She paused. "This Lodovico is a proper man."

Emilia smiled faintly. "A very handsome man."

"He speaks well."

"I know a lady in Venice," Emilia said archly, "who would have walked barefoot to Palestine for a touch of his nether lip."

Desdemona laughed — and then, quite without transition, began to sing.

"The poor soul sat singing by a sycamore tree,
Sing all a green willow…"
Emilia's hands slowed.

"Her hand on her bosom, her head on her knee,
Sing willow, willow, willow…"
The tune, sweet and winding, filled the room with a quiet grief.

"The fresh streams ran by her, and murmur'd her moans,
Sing willow, willow, willow…"

Desdemona paused, her voice thickening.

"Her salt tears fell from her, and soften'd the stones…"

She trailed off, folding a ribbon between her fingers.

"Lay by these…"

She shook her head, then sang again — softly now.

"Sing willow, willow, willow… Prithee hie thee, he'll come anon."

Her voice caught on the next line, and she stammered:

"Sing all a green willow must be my garland…"

She stopped again, as though the meaning had struck her afresh.

"Let nobody blame him," she murmured, her voice no longer in song. "His scorn I approve…"

Then, with sudden sharpness, she flinched. "Nay — that's not next—"

She turned her head quickly, listening.

"Hark!" she whispered. "Who is't that knocks?"

And so the song ended — unfinished.

Emilia, standing half in shadow, cocked her head toward the sound. "It's the wind," she said, though her tone suggested she wasn't entirely sure. Desdemona had stilled mid-song, one finger resting on her temple.

Then, softly, she resumed:

"I called my love false love,"
"But what said he then?"
"Sing willow, willow, willow…"
"If I court more women, you'll couch with more men."
She broke off, smiling bitterly. "So, get thee gone. Good night."

Her hand moved again to her face.

"Ay me, my eyes do itch… Doth that bode weeping?"

"'Tis neither here nor there," said Emilia.

"I have heard it said so," Desdemona murmured. Then, in a breathless hush: "O, these men, these men!"

There was silence for a beat, then Desdemona turned.

"Dost thou in conscience think — tell me, Emilia — that there be women do abuse their husbands in such gross kind?"

Emilia shrugged, gently. "There be some such, no question."

Desdemona's voice softened, incredulous. "Wouldst thou do such a deed for all the world?"

Emilia turned from the fire and gave a sidelong glance.

"Why, would not you?"

"No," Desdemona said, shocked. "By this heavenly light!"

Emilia grinned. "Nor I neither — by this heavenly light. I might do't as well i' the dark."

Desdemona laughed faintly, despite herself. "Wouldst thou do such a deed for all the world?"

Emilia moved closer, her voice dry. "The world's a huge thing. It is a great price for a small vice."

"In truth," said Desdemona, "I think thou wouldst not."

"In truth," said Emilia, "I think I should — and undo't when I had done. Marry, I would not do such a thing for a joint-ring, nor for measures of lawn, nor for gowns, petticoats, nor caps — nor any petty exhibition."

She turned and faced her mistress squarely.

"But for the whole world — why, who would not make her husband a cuckold to make him a monarch? I should venture purgatory for't."

Desdemona, shocked, said, "Beshrew me, if I would do such a wrong for the whole world."

Emilia leaned on the edge of the bed, her tone matter-of-fact.

"Why, the wrong is but a wrong i' the world. And having the world for your labour, 'tis a wrong in your own world, and you might quickly make it right."

Desdemona shook her head. "I do not think there is any such woman."

Emilia snorted softly. "Yes, a dozen — and as many to the vantage as would store the world they played for."

Her voice grew sharper now — not in malice, but in clarity.

"But I do think it is their husbands' faults if wives do fall."

She stood now, gathering the garments from the floor.

"Say that they slack their duties and pour our treasures into foreign laps... or else break out in peevish jealousies, throwing restraint upon us; or say they strike us, or scant our former having in despite;"

There was nothing mad in her tone, nothing unwholesome. If anything, it was the world that seemed ill — not the women struggling to survive inside it.

She turned again, and her eyes, in that moment, were bright and dangerous.

"We have galls, madam — and though we have some grace, yet have we some revenge."

She moved closer, her voice low but ringing.

"Let husbands know their wives have sense like them — they see, and smell, and have their palates both for sweet and sour, as husbands have."

Desdemona sat in silence, watching her.

"What is it that they do when they change us for others?" Emilia asked. "Is it sport? I think it is. And doth affection breed it? I think it doth. Is't frailty that thus errs? It is so too."

Then, with a final wave of the hand:

"And have not we affections? Desires for sport? Frailty, as men have? Then let them use us well — else let them know: the ills we do, their ills instruct us so."

Desdemona, moved but not shaken, rose.

"Good night, good night. Heaven me such uses send — not to pick bad from bad, but by bad mend!"

And with that, the two women retired — one dreaming of reconciliation, the other of reckoning — both unaware that the end had already drawn breath.

ACT V

The Bed and the Grave

In which the night devours the heart, the truth comes too late, and the stars close their eyes.

ACT V SCENE 1

The street was narrow, twisting like a broken limb through the sleeping quarters of war-battered Cyprus. The hour lay in that cold hush between midnight and resurrection, when even the rats scurried softer and the oil-lamps—starved of wicks and weary of their flame—guttered against walls pocked with salt and musket fire. A pall of gunpowder clung to the stones, not fresh, and mingled with sweat and sea air, and something sourer: the scent of fear long past and still unresolved.

There, where the alleyway buckled into shadow behind a grocer's abandoned bulk-cart—its wheels long since surrendered to rust—two figures crept. One wore a cloak of deception. The other wore fear like a fevered child wears a blanket.

"Here," whispered Iago, beckoning Roderigo behind the cart as though inviting him into the vestibule of some foul church, "stand firm. He'll be here anon."

Roderigo's breath steamed in the air. His hand trembled upon the hilt of his rapier, which was half-drawn and wholly unsure.

Iago, eyes glinting like the eyes of a candlelit eel, gave him the words he needed like a priest administering poison instead of sacrament.

"Draw your blade fully. And when he comes—strike home. Quick, quick now. There's naught to fear while I'm at your elbow. This either makes us... or unmakes us entirely."

He clapped Roderigo on the back and melted into the darkness like ink into black blotting paper.

Left alone, the would-be assassin shifted his weight from foot to foot like a schoolboy outside a headmaster's door.

"I've no great appetite for murder," he muttered, as though hoping his own conscience might overhear and go easier on him in the reckoning. "Yet... he gave me reason. He's but a man gone."

He unsheathed his sword with a hiss—too loud in that breathless place. The tip shook.

"Forth, my sword," he said, trying to speak it brave. "He dies."

Elsewhere, Iago watched. His mind, a cathedral of wickedness, sang its own psalm: I've pricked this young fool near to bursting. He's angry now... ripe for slaughter. Whether he kills Cassio or Cassio him—or if both perish together— Every way makes my gain. Should Roderigo live, he'll demand back the gold and jewels that I bobb'd from him as 'gifts' for Desdemona, poor simpleton. No, no. He must not live. Nor Cassio neither. The man has a daily beauty in his life that makes me ugly. If he lives, the Moor may unfold me to him; there stand I in much peril. No, both must die.

And just then, footfalls on the cobbles.

Cassio emerged—a soldier at ease, whistling under his breath the tune of some bawdy mess-hall ditty. His stride was steady, the walk of a man who feared no shadows, though perhaps he should.

Roderigo lunged from the dark with a cry that was half fury, half apology.

"Villain! Thou diest!" The point of Roderigo's rapier struck with a heavy thwack, grazing leather, biting into the wool below—but not piercing flesh.

Cassio parried by instinct—his sword not yet drawn, but his body taught from years of drill. Though his reputation marked him more courtly than combat-born, his training ran deep, and his dress that night betrayed quiet readiness. Over his doublet he wore a well-fitted buff jerkin—stitched oxhide, supple but dense, darkened by wear and the oil of maintenance. Beneath, a double-padded gambeson of wool and linen, quilted tight, built not for show but survival.

"That thrust had been my enemy indeed… But that my coat is better than thou know'st,"Cassio now smiled in the dark, though it was more of a feeling than something seen. He was not afraid, and indeed he knew how to handle himself, even enjoyed a good bit of sport. "Now, let us see how yours fares!" he challenged.

With a soldier's fluidity, he drew, riposted, and skewered Roderigo in the side. The youth staggered, bleeding, whimpering.

"O, I am slain!" he gasped, though in truth his current wound was not fatal.

But then, from behind, a snake struck.

A blade—short, precise, and cruel—slashed across the back of Cassio's leg—finding the flesh behind the knee. It was a butcher's cut: swift, precise, disabling. He cried out, fell like a wounded stag, and began to crawl, dragging blood behind him like a tide turned red. "I am maim'd forever! Help! Ho! Murder! Murder!"

Iago, already disappearing into the night, left behind a tableau of agony and iron. Othello entered then, drawn by the clamour. His steps were soft, his gaze fixed. A man already half-mad with conviction, half-drunk on imagined betrayal.

"The voice of Cassio," he breathed. "Iago keeps his word."

He did not rush to help, but stood like a ghost watching his own funeral. He also heard Roderigo crying out, sputtering "O, villain that I am…"

"'Tis even so."

Cassio cried out again, his voice cracking with pain.

"Help! Light! A surgeon!"

And Othello, grim with his resolve, whispered into the shadows:

"O brave Iago. Honest and just. You've avenged me, taught me—yes, taught me well. Minion,"—he said it as though spitting out the last of love—"your dear lies dead. Your unblest fate hastens. Strumpet, I come. From my heart, I tear the charm your eyes once cast. Your bed, stained by lust, shall be stained anew—with blood."

With that, he vanished like the tide retreating before a storm, another shadow merging with the dark.

Presently, Lodovico and Gratiano came ambling through the night, lanternless but murmuring concern. They were men of noble birth but minor mind, and they moved like clerks through a riot—too cautious, too late.

"Murder!" cried Cassio again.

Gratiano paused. "Hark! A cry most dire."

Roderigo gasped from the ground, blood bubbling in his throat.

"O wretched villain!" he moaned—not quite for Cassio, and not quite for himself, but for some indistinct notion of justice long since miscarried.

The two noblemen stalled. "Two or three groan: it is a heavy night." They did not rush to help though, like prey at the smell of blood.

"These may be counterfeits," said Lodovico, looking about with a senator's caution. "Let's not step into the cry without more help."

Roderigo coughed. "Nobody come? Then shall I bleed to death." He was sobbing now, truly pathetic, all his hurts and injustices stinging in his blindness that black night. And then came Iago again, torch in one hand, sword in the other, his shirt untucked and face contorted into that perfect mask of concern he wore so well.

"Who's there?" he called, light flaring across the stone. "Whose noise is this that ones on murder?"

Lodovico spoke, his voice a loud urgent whisper "We do not know."

Iago retorted loudly and with a ferocious pretence at care for others "Did not you hear a cry?"

Cassio, somehow steeling his voice, called out from the dark, "Here, here! for heaven's sake, help me!"

Iago advanced. His eyes swept the scene: Roderigo clutching his belly, Cassio clutching his leg, the nobility clutching their scruples. He knelt beside Cassio, torchlight dancing in his eyes like devils in a cathedral.

"What's the matter?" he asked. But he already knew.

Cassio lay amid the street's grime and blood, half propped against the stone wall, eyes rolling, leg unstrung like a haunch for market, lips peeled back with pain like a man trying to swallow his own scream. From the shadows came voices, feet hurrying now.

Gratiano blinked at him, "This is Othello's ancient, as I take it."

"The same indeed," Lodovico replied, stepping forward. "A very valiant fellow."

It was a cruel comedy. For there stood Iago—handsome, breathless, shirt stained with the sweat of orchestrated chaos—blinking as though he'd stumbled upon the scene by accident.

"What's this?" he asked, his tone sculpted from earnest confusion. "Who cries so grievously?"

Cassio lifted his head, his breath rattling, his damaged leg like an anchor to his own misfortune and betrayal.

"Iago?" he gasped. "O—I am undone… spoil'd… villains, Iago—give me some help!"

The look of shocked affection that Iago cast upon him might've won him sainthood in less discerning company. He fell to his knees beside the wounded former lieutenant, clucking like a nursemaid, all tremor and concern.

"O me, lieutenant! What villains have done this?"

Cassio's face twisted. "One… I think… is still hereabout and cannot make away."

Iago sprang up, sword out, eyes sweeping the shadows like a man possessed. "O treacherous villains!" he spat to the night. "What men are these? Come out—come help!"

From the shadows, a weak voice: "O… help me here…"

"That's one of them!" Cassio growled, struggling to rise, pointing to the quivering mass that was Roderigo. And Iago, moved by the terrible theatre of the moment, drew near Roderigo and looked into the dying man's eyes with something almost like pity.

"O murderous slave," he said. Then, swiftly, with the efficiency of a butcher at dawn—he plunged his blade into Roderigo's chest.

Roderigo's cry tore the night open.

"O damn'd Iago! O… inhuman dog—!"

It was almost tender, the way Iago closed the boy's eyes.

"Kill men i' the dark?" he bellowed then, rising to rally the world. "Where be these bloody thieves? Ho! Murder! MURDER!"

He turned on Lodovico and Gratiano, who stood dumbstruck. "What are you? Speak! Are you of good or ill?"

Lodovico, blinking at the absurdity of the question, answered with noble disdain:

"As you shall prove us, praise us."

Iago stepped closer, squinting theatrically.

"Signior Lodovico?"

"He, sir."

"Ah, I cry you mercy. Here lies Cassio—hurt by villains." Iago spat the word villains, though it was more noble than the traitorous truth of the situation that he had orchestrated. He had used his pawn to take down a knight.

Gratiano, bending to peer closer, gasped. "Cassio!"

Iago, kneeling once more, pressed his sleeve to Cassio's wound. "How is't, brother?"

"My leg," Cassio whispered, pale as parchment. "Cut in two…"

"Marry, heaven forbid," Iago murmured, and tore the linen from his shirt to bind the wound. "Light, gentlemen, lend me light!"

A small crowd was gathering now, and soldiers had arrived to keep the peace. And as if summoned by the chorus of false virtue, a new voice rang out, high and wild with terror.

"What is the matter? Who is't that cried?" It was Bianca.

She ran to Cassio's side, skirts whipping the filth, her breath catching as she saw the blood.

"O my dear Cassio! My sweet Cassio! O Cassio—Cassio—!"

Iago turned to her with a sneer just shy of sanctimony.

"O notable strumpet…"

Bianca blinked, confused, as he continued, addressing the crowd.

"Cassio, do you know who did this? Who led you thus?"

"No," Cassio croaked, lost in agony.

Gratiano stepped forward. "I was searching for you. I came too late."

Iago turned his head, solemn as a judge. "Lend me a garter—so. And fetch a chair! We must move him."

Bianca wailed, grasping at Cassio's hand. "He faints! O Cassio—Cassio—Cassio!"

Iago rose slowly, and now his performance soared.

"Gentlemen," he said gravely, "I do suspect this... trash," he gestured to Bianca without meeting her eyes, "to be a party in this injury."

Bianca gasped—truly gasped, with that purity only the falsely accused can summon.

"Patience, good Cassio," Iago soothed, kneeling beside Roderigo's corpse. He tilted the young man's chin up to the flickering light.

"Lend me your torch," he whispered. "Know we this face?"

And then, a small gasp of mock recognition: "Alas... my friend... my dear countryman—Roderigo? No... yes—O heaven! Roderigo!"

Gratiano, aghast, stepped closer. "What? Of Venice?"

"Even he, sir. Did you know him?"

"Ay," said Gratiano, his voice thickening. "Too well."

Iago turned his eyes on Gratiano. "Signior Gratiano?" He bowed, almost piously. "I cry your gentle pardon. These... bloody accidents must excuse my manners, that so neglected you."

"I'm glad to see you," Gratiano said, still trying to make sense of the carnage.

"How do you, Cassio?" Iago called, louder now, as men brought a chair into view. "A chair, a chair!"

"Roderigo?" Gratiano asked again, as if hoping it were some other corpse.

"Ay," said Iago. "He. He 'tis he."

Two soldiers raised Cassio carefully into the chair, his face contorted into a grimace of pain. One pressed a cloth to his thigh. Another murmured a prayer.

Gratiano stepped back, breathless. "Some good man—bear him carefully from hence. I'll fetch the general's surgeon."

He turned to Bianca, who knelt weeping beside the broken lieutenant. "And you, mistress—spare your labour. He who lies slain there, Cassio, was my dear friend."

Bianca looked up, streaked with tears.

"What malice," Gratiano asked, "was between you?"

And in the stillness that followed—blood drying on cobblestone, men murmuring, a woman sobbing into her skirts—Iago stood like a saint atop a pyre.

Unburned. Unchallenged.

And entirely in control.

Cassio, slumped in his blood-streaked chair, gritted his teeth against the pain.

"None in the world," he groaned, "nor do I know the man."

Iago turned to Bianca with a flourish so false it shone like cheap gold in torchlight.

"Look at her, gentlemen," he said, gesturing with the ease of a snake oil preacher. "Look how pale. See the gastness of her eye. You'd think the ghost of guilt had just risen up and stared her down."

Bianca blinked furiously, caught between disbelief and indignation.

"Look well upon her," Iago pressed on. "Do you not see it? Her gaze betrays her. Guiltiness will speak, gentlemen, even if all tongues were struck dumb."

He was a showman now—commanding the stage, his voice a subtle whip, his manner pious yet pitiless.

But then—

"'Las, what's the matter?" called a familiar voice from beyond the torch-glow.

Emilia, breathless and dishevelled, pushed through the gathering crowd like a woman summoned by God to correct a wicked sermon. Her eyes found her husband's first.

"What's the matter, husband?"

Iago rose to meet her, voice low and grim.

"Cassio was set upon, in the dark. Roderigo led it. Others were with him, but they've escaped. Cassio's near death. Roderigo... is gone."

Emilia gasped. "Alas, good gentleman! Alas, good Cassio!"

And Iago, with the cruelty of a man who cannot resist a final lash, turned to Bianca once more, as though proving a theorem of the flesh.

"This, Emilia," he said, voice oily, "this is the fruit of whoring. Go, ask Cassio where he supp'd tonight."

He turned to Bianca with mock surprise. "What, do you shake at that?"

Bianca, lips trembling but proud, lifted her chin. "He supp'd at my house—but I therefore shake not."

"O," Iago said slowly, as though a great revelation had descended, "did he so? Then I charge you: go with me."

But before he could turn, Emilia stepped between them like a knife drawn for honour.

"Fie upon thee, strumpet!" she hissed.

Bianca reeled, wounded not by guilt, but by the injustice of the blow.

"I am no strumpet," she said quietly. "But of life as honest as you that thus abuse me."

Emilia scoffed. "As I? Foh. Fie upon thee!"

Iago raised his hands, as if to break a fight in a brothel—ever the noble servant.

"Kind gentlemen," he said, addressing the assembled crowd, "let's see poor Cassio dressed and bound. Come, mistress. You must tell us another tale, I think."

He placed a firm hand upon Bianca's shoulder. Not unkindly. Not kindly either. The grip of ownership, of disposal.

Then he turned to Emilia.

"Run you to the citadel. Wake the general. Tell my lord and lady what has happened this night."

Emilia hesitated, then ran.

Iago lingered, watching her disappear into the dark with his eyes half-lidded, his face unreadable.

"Will you go on?" he asked the others, ushering them after her, like sheep toward a cliff's edge.

Then, lowering his voice so none but the shadows might hear, he muttered:

"This is the night that either makes me… or fordoes me quite." He was enjoying himself thoroughly. And with that, he passed into the dark, leaving the street as it was found: Empty. Blood-slick. Silent but for the slow drip of justice still withheld.

ACT V SCENE 2

The air in the bedchamber was stilled, thick with the perfume of lavender water and extinguished candles. A single lamp remained, burning low on the far wall. Its flame trembled, casting slow circles upon the ceiling like a soul reluctant to leave the world. And there upon the bed, veiled in linen and moonlight, lay Desdemona.

She slept as the innocent sleep, one hand curled like a lily beneath her cheek, her chest rising and falling with the gentle rhythm of trust. Her breath was soft as silk drawn through fingers, and her face—as pale as the marble saints of San Marco—bore no trace of the storm that now pressed against the door. That door creaked. Slowly. And into the hush came Othello. He entered like a man walking into his own tomb. Each step echoed with the weight of irrevocable intention. His sword was sheathed; the murder he meant was not the kind that war teaches. It was quiet, private—a matter between breath and pillow.

"It is the cause," he whispered, eyes fixed upon her sleeping form. "It is the cause, my soul…"

His voice was hoarse, but reverent. He spoke not to Desdemona, but to some unseen court of conscience, or to the stars themselves—those chaste and distant witnesses.

"Let me not name it to you, you chaste stars! It is the cause."

He moved closer, and the candlelight caught the curve of his jaw, the glint of moisture at the corner of his eye. His hand brushed the edge of the coverlet.

"Yet I'll not shed her blood," he said, more to himself than to God. "Nor scar that whiter skin of hers than snow, and smooth as monumental alabaster…"

There was awe in his voice, and agony.

"Yet she must die, else she'll betray more men."

A silence. He stared at the flickering lamp.

"Put out the light, and then put out the light…"

He took the lamp in hand. Held it high. Then slowly turned it down, extinguishing the flame with a final hiss.

"If I quench thee, thou flaming minister, I can again thy former light restore, should I repent me…"

He stared at the darkness, as if testing that claim.

"But once put out thy light, thou cunning'st pattern of excelling nature, I know not where is that Promethean heat that can thy light relume."

He turned back to Desdemona. His hands trembled. He knelt beside the bed and pressed his lips to her shoulder. Her skin was warm.

"When I have pluck'd the rose, I cannot give it vital growth again. It must needs wither. I'll smell it on the tree." He bent forward and kissed her. "Ah, balmy breath, that dost almost persuade justice to break her sword!" Another kiss. And then a third. "One more. One more. Be thus when thou art dead, and I will kill thee, and love thee after. One more—and this the last…"

His voice cracked.

"So sweet was ne'er so fatal…"

Tears streaked down his cheeks. His face contorted with sorrow's strangest symmetry—grief and love, fury and awe.

"I must weep," he said, "but they are cruel tears. This sorrow's heavenly; it strikes where it doth love."

And just then, she stirred. A gentle shift beneath the sheets, like the sea catching its breath.

"Who's there?" she murmured, eyes fluttering open. "Othello?"

He knelt beside her, his face half-shadowed.

"Ay, Desdemona."

She smiled faintly, still half dreaming. "Will you come to bed, my lord?"

There was silence.

Then he asked—too quietly— "Have you pray'd tonight, Desdemona?"

Her brow furrowed, the sleep drifting from her eyes like mist from glass.

"Ay, my lord."

Othello looked away. His throat moved as he swallowed.

"If you bethink yourself of any crime… unreconciled as yet to heaven and grace… solicit for it straight."

Desdemona sat up now, pulling the coverlet to her chest.

"Alas, my lord… what do you mean by that?"

He rose, pacing to the far side of the room.

"Well, do it," he said. "And be brief. I will walk by."

She stared after him, confused and afraid.

"I would not kill thy unprepared spirit," he muttered. "No. Heaven forfend. I would not kill thy soul."

Her voice cracked. "Talk you of killing?"

"Ay," said Othello. "I do."

"Then heaven have mercy on me!"

"Amen," he said. "With all my heart."

She rose from the bed now, trembling. "If you say so… I hope you will not kill me."

He said nothing. Only watched her, his face unreadable.

"And yet… I fear you," she whispered. "You are fatal then, when your eyes roll so."

She stepped closer.

"Why I should fear, I know not—since guiltiness I know not. But yet… I feel I fear."

Othello's jaw tightened.

"Think on thy sins," he said.

"They are loves I bear to you."

"Ay," he said. "And for that thou diest."

She stepped back, horror blooming.

"That death's unnatural that kills for loving…"

He gnawed his lower lip, his body trembling. A man possessed by a spirit darker than himself.

"Alas," she whispered, "why gnaw you so your nether lip?"

A strange stillness overtook him.

"Some bloody passion shakes your very frame," she said. "These are portents…"

She paused. Her voice softened, became smaller.

"But yet… I hope, I hope… they do not point on me."

Othello turned from the edge of tears, from mercy's precipice, and hardened himself anew. His face drew taut like a curtain before a tragedy.

"Peace," he said, voice low, shaking. "Be still."

Desdemona, startled, nodded. "I will so. What's the matter?"

And then, at last, he named it—the wound at the centre of this fevered world:

"That handkerchief… which I so loved, and gave thee— Thou gav'st to Cassio."

She recoiled as if struck by madness clothed in a lover's voice.

"No, by my life and soul!" she cried. "Send for the man, and ask him!"

But Othello only stared, death blooming behind his eyes like frost on a mirror.

"Sweet soul," he said, and there was something almost tender in the way the words turned against themselves, "take heed… take heed of perjury. Thou art on thy deathbed."

A beat.

Desdemona looked at him, uncomprehending.

"Ay," she said, voice rising, "but not yet to die."

"Yes," he said. "Presently."

And then, suddenly, the soldier was back—the general. Firm, final.

"Confess thee freely of thy sin. For to deny each article with oath cannot remove… nor choke the strong conception that I do groan withal. Thou art to die."

Desdemona backed toward the bed, the curtain's edge gathered in her fists like a lifeline.

"Then… Lord have mercy on me."

"I say amen."

She reached for him.

"And have you mercy too!" she cried. "I never did offend you in my life. Never loved Cassio… but with such general courtesy as heaven allows!"

"I never gave him token," she whispered.

But it was as if she were speaking to stone.

"By heaven," he growled, "I saw my handkerchief in's hand. O perjured woman! Thou dost stone my heart…."

His voice was breaking now with the unbearable tension of loving what he must destroy.

"Thou makest me call what I intend to do a murder—which I thought a sacrifice."

He turned away, jaw clenched. "I saw the handkerchief."

She clutched the bedpost now, her knuckles bloodless. "He found it then," she said. "I never gave it him. Send for him. Let him confess the truth!"

Othello turned slowly.

"He hath confess'd."

Her knees gave slightly, but she caught herself.

"What, my lord?"

"That he hath used thee."

"How?" she breathed. "Unlawfully?"

"Ay."

She shook her head violently. "He will not say so."

"No," said Othello. "His mouth is stopp'd. Honest Iago… hath taken order for't."

A terrible silence bloomed in the room.

"O!" Desdemona cried. "My fear interprets… What? Is he dead?"

The word hit like a thunderclap, and all the stars in Desdemona's sky seemed to go out.

"Had all his hairs been lives," said Othello coldly, "my great revenge had stomach for them all."

Desdemona crumpled.

"Alas," she whispered. "He is betray'd… and I undone."

Othello stared down at her, seeing not a wife, but a symbol, a wound, a flame.

"Out, strumpet!" he roared, voice cracking. "Weep'st thou for him to my face?"

She fell to her knees.

"O—banish me, my lord. But kill me not!"

"Down, strumpet!"

"Kill me tomorrow! Let me live tonight!"

"Nay, if you strive—"

"But half an hour!"

"Being done… there is no pause."

"But while I say one prayer—"

"It is too late."

He moved forward. She screamed. And then—silence. He stifled her. With hands that once held her like a relic, he now held her as a weight to be dropped. It was not sudden. It was slow, the labour of a man who believed he was doing right, even as everything in him wept and shattered and pleaded for time to turn back. The bed shifted under their weight. The sheets writhed. Her fingers clawed briefly at the air. And then— nothing. Othello staggered back. The room was deathly still, save for his breath: ragged, hollow, the breath of a man exiled from his own soul. The lamp guttered. Outside, unseen, a gull cried over the sea. The silence that followed her smothering was monstrous. It rang with its own sound—a silence that echoed, that roared in the ears. Othello staggered back, face glazed, the weight of what he had done falling like chainmail over his limbs.

Then—a voice from beyond the door.

"My lord! My lord! What, ho! My lord, my lord!"

Othello flinched, caught halfway between resolve and recoil. He turned sharply, eyes drawn back to the bed. Desdemona had not gone still after all.

There—beneath the gauze of moonlight—her body stirred. A soft, broken sound came from her lips. Not a word. Not even a breath, exactly. More a choking cough, rough and wet, as though her throat were trying to remember how to speak through the ruin left in its place. Her fingers twitched on the coverlet. One foot shifted beneath the sheet. Her lips parted in that ghastly effort of survival—the gasp of a soul clinging by the slenderest thread. Othello staggered back a pace, staring.

"Not dead?" he breathed. "Not yet quite dead?"

He stood over her, torn and trembling. The weight of mercy now a sharper thing than vengeance.

"I," he whispered, his voice raw with conflict, "that am cruel… am yet merciful."

He knelt beside her again. His hands moved toward her—those hands that once stroked her cheek as though she were made of breath and blessing. Now they hovered like the hands of a man about to snap the neck of a bird too broken to fly. Her eyes fluttered. Unfocused. Afraid.

"I would not have thee linger in thy pain," he murmured, as if pleading with heaven for permission. "So. So…"

His fingers moved toward her throat—

"What, ho! My lord, my lord!"

He froze. The knock came louder now. Urgent. Human. Othello's hands withdrew as though scorched. He turned sharply from the bed, reeling like a drunk from revelation. He was not done, and yet the world insisted upon its entry.

"Who's there?" he called, breathlessly.

And from beyond the door: Emilia's voice—clearer now, more determined.

"O good my lord, I would speak a word with you!"

Othello swallowed hard.

"Yes," he muttered, staggering to his feet. "'Tis Emilia. By and by."

He turned back to Desdemona, who now lay still again—too still?

"She's dead," he told himself. "'Tis like she comes to speak of Cassio's death…"

He stared down at the twisted sheets.

"The noise was here," he whispered. "Ha… no more moving?"

He stepped closer, peering. "Still as the grave…"

His mouth twitched, uncertain. "Shall she come in? Were't good?"

He studied the body—again unsure.

"I think she stirs again…"

A long pause.

"No."

He shook his head. "What's best to do?"

His gaze fixed on the body.

"If she come in, she'll sure speak to my wife…"

His voice cracked.

"My wife? My wife!—what wife?"

A sound escaped him—some beast's groan torn from the belly of a man.

"I have no wife."

He staggered against the bedpost.

"O insupportable! O heavy hour!"

He looked to the window, to the pale moon, the quivering stars.

"Methinks it should be now a huge eclipse, of sun and moon, and that the affrighted globe should yawn at alteration."

Emilia's voice came again.

"I do beseech you—let me speak with you! O good my lord!"

Othello blinked as though waking from a dream, and drew his sword absently, some battle reflex, or a child hugging its favourite trinket.

"I had forgot thee," he murmured. "O, come in, Emilia. Soft—by and by. Let me the curtains draw."

He crossed the room like a man underwater, turned the key, and opened the door. She rushed in, skirts snapping like sails in the storm-wind of her alarm.

"What's the matter with thee now?" he asked.

Emilia's face was grey with horror.

"O, my good lord," she gasped. "Yonder's foul murder done!"

He stiffened. "What now?"

"But now, my lord!"

Othello shook his head slowly, the storm inside gathering once more.

"It is the very error of the moon," he said. "She comes more nearer earth than she was wont… and makes men mad."

Emilia backed a step, unsettled.

"No, my lord. Cassio… Cassio hath kill'd a young Venetian. Call'd Roderigo."

Othello froze. His blood turned to ice.

"Roderigo… kill'd? And Cassio?" he asked, the hope souring already.

"No. Cassio is not kill'd."

Othello staggered.

"Not Cassio killed? Then murder's out of tune. And sweet revenge… grows harsh."

And then—a sound.

Not a word. Not a cry. But a sound no longer living and yet not quite dead. It came like a ghost dragged back into the body by some final, misbegotten mercy. A gurgling breath clawed its way up through the ruin of her throat. A broken rasp—as though her soul, snagged on splinters of cartilage and sinew, refused to depart cleanly. It was a sound choked in its birth, like water trying to speak. Then, with a great effort—her chest heaving once, then again—she forced the words through the shattered instrument of her voice:

"O… falsely… falsely… murder'd…"

Each syllable tore itself from her as if it carried fragments of her lungs with it.

Emilia gasped, hand flying to her breast as though struck.

"Alas!" she cried. "What cry is that?"

Othello staggered, blinking in horror. "That? What?"

"Out and alas!" Emilia shrieked. "That was my lady's voice!"

She ran to the bed. The moment her eyes fell on the ruin there, she collapsed beside it, skirts tumbling, arms already reaching.

"Help! Help, ho! Help! O lady, speak again! Sweet Desdemona! O sweet mistress, speak!"

And Desdemona—eyes flickering like the last flame in a winded lamp—opened her mouth again. Her lips moved, cracked and bloodless. The sound that came was smaller now, a dry whisper, shaped more by breath than voice.

"A guiltless death I die."

It was spoken like confession and absolution both.

Emilia fell across her, pressing her cheek to Desdemona's brow, whispering back through tears, "O, who hath done this deed?"

There was a pause. A pause that stretched the span between one world and the next. And then, one last breath. A final coil of air, expelled in agony and love entwined. She did not speak the words so much as offer them—like the final petal from a plucked rose:

"Nobody. I myself. Farewell. Commend me to my kind lord…O… farewell…"

The last syllable shuddered in her throat, and then died. Her head rolled slightly to one side. A tremor passed through her lips—as though her body, reluctant to stop loving, had not yet informed her that she could love no more.

Then—silence.

The kind of silence that makes the walls lean in.

The kind of silence that never leaves a room.

Her soul, if such things could be seen, might have looked like a dove that had flown through smoke. Startled. Scorched. But free.

She died.

Othello stood frozen. His face blank. The sword he still held, limp by his side.

"Why—how should she be murdered?" he asked, like a schoolboy caught at mischief.

Emilia, horror spreading, whispered, "Alas… who knows?"

"You heard her say herself," he said too quickly, "it was not I."

"She said so," Emilia replied. "I must needs report the truth."

Then Othello stepped into the void entirely.

"She's, like a liar, gone to burning hell. 'Twas I that kill'd her."

Emilia turned, eyes wide, as if the Devil himself had whispered behind her.

"O," she said. "The more angel she… and you the blacker devil."

Othello staggered toward her, eyes blazing.

"She turn'd to folly. She was a whore."

"Thou dost belie her," said Emilia, steel in her voice now. "And thou art a devil."

"She was false as water."

"Thou art rash as fire, to say she was false!" Emilia roared. "O, she was heavenly true!"

Othello raised his hand—but could not strike her.

"Cassio did top her," he said. "Ask thy husband else. I were damn'd beneath all depth in hell… But that I did proceed upon just grounds. Thy husband knew it all."

There was silence. The kind before eruption.

Emilia stared at him.

"My husband?"

"Ay," said Othello.

"That she was false to wedlock?"

"Ay. With Cassio."

She shook her head like a woman waking from a long, cruel dream.

"Nay," he added, "had she been true… if heaven would make me such another world—of one entire and perfect chrysolite—I'd not have sold her for it."

Emilia took one step back, her voice breaking into thunder.

"My husband?!"

"Ay," said Othello. "'Twas he that told me first. An honest man he is—and hates the slime that sticks on filthy deeds."

"My husband…" she whispered.

"What needs this iteration, woman?" he barked. "I say thy husband!"

Then her whole body seemed to rise up with the fury of a betrayed world.

"O mistress," she cried, turning to Desdemona's still form, "villainy hath made mocks with love!"

And then—like a sword finally drawn—

"My husband… say that she was false?!"

Othello stood in the centre of the room, face mottled by the shifting light. Emilia towered before him, all fire and grief, a woman who had nothing left but truth—and the courage to speak it.

"It was he," said Othello, voice distant, drowning. "I say thy husband. Dost understand the word?"

He turned to her, his face twitching.

"My friend. Thy husband. Honest, honest Iago."

Emilia recoiled, as if the name burned her.

"If he say so," she hissed, "may his pernicious soul rot half a grain a day!"

Her eyes flared wide. Her breath came fast.

"He lies to the heart," she spat. "She was too fond… too kind… too faithful—to her most filthy bargain."

Othello's lip curled, and he pointed at her with the blade he still clutched. "Ha?"

Emilia stepped closer, "Do thy worst!" She met his eyes. There was no tremor in her voice. "This deed of thine is no more worthy heaven than thou wast worthy her!"

"Peace," Othello growled. "You were best in silence keep."

But Emilia would not be silenced. Her grief had made her fearless. Her voice rang like a bell in a fire-ravaged city.

"Thou hast not half that power to do me harm as I have to be hurt!"

She stepped into his space—unarmed, unyielding.

"O gull! O dolt! As ignorant as dirt!"

She pointed at Desdemona's still form.

"Thou hast done a deed—!"

Othello raised his sword, but Emilia did not flinch.

"I care not for thy sword! I'll make thee known, even if I lose twenty lives!"

And then she turned from him and screamed to the world:

"Help! Help, ho! Help! The Moor hath kill'd my mistress! Murder! Murder!"

The door burst open—soldiers poured in like judgment itself: Montano, Gratiano, and Iago at their head.

"What is the matter?" barked Montano. "How now, General?!"

But Emilia ignored him. Her eyes had locked on Iago—her husband, her deceiver.

"O!" she cried. "Are you come, Iago? You've done well—very well—that men must lay their murders on your neck!"

Gratiano stepped forward. "What is the matter?"

Emilia turned on him, eyes wild, voice shaking.

"Disprove this villain, if thou be'st a man!" she howled. "He says thou told'st him that his wife was false!"

She jabbed a finger toward Iago. "I know thou didst not! Thou art not such a villain!"

She shook. Her voice cracked. "Speak! For my heart is full."

Iago looked her in the eye, calm as a stone in the tide.

"I told him what I thought," he said flatly. "And told no more than what he found himself was apt and true."

Emilia's mouth opened. She stepped back as though struck.

"But… did you ever tell him she was false?"

"I did," said Iago, unblinking.

Then Emilia let loose a cry that shook the timbers.

"You told a lie! An odious, damnèd lie! Upon my soul, a lie—a wicked lie!" She turned to the others, desperate. "She false with Cassio?! Did you say with Cassio?!"

"With Cassio, mistress," Iago sneered. "Go to—charm your tongue."

But Emilia—O brave Emilia—lifted her chin.

"I will not charm my tongue," she said. "I am bound to speak."

She turned back to the room, the body, the blood.

"My mistress lies murder'd in her bed."

Gasps rang out. One of the soldiers crossed himself.

"O heavens forfend!" someone whispered.

"And your reports," she said, staring at Iago with something like holy fury, "have set the murder on."

Othello, shoulders drooping, turned to them all like a dying man admitting his guilt at last.

"Nay… stare not, masters. It is true. Indeed."

Gratiano turned pale. "'Tis… a strange truth."

"A monstrous act," Montano muttered.

And Emilia—

"Villany, villany, villany!" she roared, like one possessed. "I think upon't—I think—I smell it! O villany!"

She clutched her chest. Her knees buckled.

"I thought so then—I'll kill myself for grief!" And again— "O villany! Villany!"

Iago stepped forward swiftly, hand half to his dagger.

"What, are you mad? I charge you—get you home."

But Emilia turned to the men.

"Good gentlemen," she said, voice shaking but firm, "let me have leave to speak. 'Tis proper I obey him—but not now."

She turned to Iago, and for the first time in her life, looked at him with absolute clarity.

"Perchance, Iago," she said softly, "I will ne'er go home."

Then—Othello groaned.

It was no word—no human sound. Just anguish, the raw howl of a man dragging his own soul behind him. He stumbled. Fell face-first onto the bed beside Desdemona.

"O! O! O!"

Emilia turned to him and said with the quiet bitterness of truth made flesh:

"Nay, lay thee down and roar. For thou hast kill'd the sweetest innocent that e'er did lift up eye."

Othello rose, slow and unsteady, like Lazarus from a grave too shallow.

"O… she was foul," he rasped.

"I scarce did know you, uncle," he added to Gratiano, the words tumbling now like stones. "There lies your niece— Whose breath… indeed… these hands have newly stopp'd."

He looked down at them—bloodless, shaking.

"I know this act shows horrible… and grim."

Gratiano stood frozen beside the bed, gazing down at the carnage, his face hollow with disbelief.

"Poor Desdemona," he murmured. "I am glad thy father's dead. Thy match was mortal to him, and pure grief tore his old thread in twain."

He glanced toward the door, as if the ghost of Brabantio might step through it, wailing.

"Had he lived to see this," Gratiano whispered, "he'd have cursed his better angel, and thrown himself from grace."

Othello stood over Desdemona like a statue cracked by lightning.

"'Tis pitiful," he muttered. "But yet—Iago knows—she did the deed with Cassio. A thousand times, he said. And she gave him the token. I saw it in his hand."

His eyes glazed.

"The handkerchief… an antique token… My father gave my mother…"

And then, from across the room—Emilia's voice, rising like judgment: "O heaven! O heavenly powers!"

Iago moved then. Quick. Too quick.

"Come, hold your peace," he hissed, stepping toward her.

But Emilia, filled with something righteous and dreadful, lifted her voice higher still: "'Twill out!" she cried. "'Twill out! I peace?! No! I will speak as liberal as the north wind!"

She turned to the others, face shining with tears, but burning with truth.

"Let heaven and men and devils—all, all, cry shame against me— yet I'll speak!"

Iago drew closer, eyes narrowed.

"Be wise," he said, voice now low, venomous. "Get you home."

"I will not," she snapped.

He moved. His hand went to his dagger.

"Fie!" Gratiano cried. "Your sword upon a woman?!"

But Iago no longer heard reason. He was already shifting— positioning himself behind her—eyes scanning the room for escape, for silence, for anything. Emilia turned again to Othello.

"O thou dull Moor!" she shouted. "That handkerchief thou speak'st of—I found it by chance! I gave it my husband. He begged me—begged me—with a solemn earnestness that far outstripped the trifle!"

Iago's face contorted.

"Villainous whore!" he spat.

"She give it to Cassio?" Emilia shouted, over him. "No, alas! I gave it to him! My husband!"

"Filth," Iago growled. "Thou liest."

"I do not!" Emilia howled. "By heaven, I do not! Gentlemen—you hear me!"

She pointed to Othello, tears streaming. "O murderous coxcomb! What should such a fool do with so good a woman?"

Othello, choking on what was left of his soul, looked to the heavens.

"Are there no stones in heaven," he bellowed, "but what serve for thunder?! Precious villain!"

He lunged.

Steel flashed.

But before he could strike—Iago acted.

Like a cornered scorpion, he turned on Emilia. Not cleanly. Not honourably. But in a rush—a coward's burst. He seized her by the arm and dragged her back—between himself and the oncoming blade. She cried out—but barely had time to finish the breath. Othello paused for a heartbeat, as Iago used his wife as a human shield, backing towards the door.

Then came the knife. Not a soldier's thrust—but a butcher's. Sudden. Dirty. From behind. A cruel, crooked entry. She buckled as it slid between her ribs. Her eyes widened—not in fear, but in betrayal. He whispered something into them—words too quiet for the others to hear. But whatever he said… silenced her. She fell. Not with dignity, but down. Folded like a thing discarded. Blood spread across the floor, staining the hem of her dress. And Iago was already gone. He slipped through the door like smoke from a snuffed flame. Gratiano rushed to Emilia's side, dropping to his knees.

"The woman falls!" he cried. "Sure—he hath kill'd his wife!"

Emilia gasped, a bubble of blood at her lips.

"Ay… ay…"

She reached blindly toward the bed.

"O… lay me by my mistress' side."

Gratiano looked up, eyes blazing.

"He's gone… but his wife's kill'd."

Montano arrived behind them, panting, blade raised.

"'Tis a notorious villain," he hissed. "Take you this weapon—" he passed Gratiano the sword he'd recovered from Othello, "—come, guard the door. Let him not pass!"

He turned, already moving.

"But kill him rather."

His voice echoed as he ran.

"I'll after that same villain—for 'tis a damned slave!"

And so the room held only the wreckage. The bed. The blood. And two women: one silenced by love, the other by treachery. Both fallen in defence of truth. The room now held the silence of aftermath. The kind of silence that does not settle, but waits. Emilia lay still beside her mistress. The final note of truth had been sung—and not even death could silence it now. Othello stood as if emptied. His eyes, once fire, were now mere smoke.

"I am not valiant neither," he said, almost to himself.

He looked down at his shaking hands, as though surprised they still obeyed him.

"But every puny whipster gets my sword. But why should honour outlive honesty? Let it go all…"

He turned, stumbling toward Emilia's body. She stirred. A low sound rose from her throat—a note of music, broken, trembling.

"What did thy song bode, lady?" she whispered toward Desdemona. "Hark… canst thou hear me?"

Her fingers twitched.

"I will play the swan," she murmured. "And die in music."

And then—so softly it seemed memory rather than voice:

"Willow… willow… willow…"

She turned her head toward the bed.

"Moor… she was chaste… she loved thee… cruel Moor…" Her voice was breaking, fading, but still it reached: "So come my soul to bliss… as I speak true…" Her hand trembled in the air. "So speaking as I think…"

She fell still.

"I die… I die."

And she was gone.

Othello turned away, face burning. He crossed the room like a man sleepwalking toward his end.

"I have another weapon in this chamber…"

He reached beneath a panel in the wall—one only a soldier would know. A hidden latch. A stored reserve. The blade glimmered like ice in firelight.

"A sword of Spain," he said. "The ice-brook's temper…"

He ran his finger down its length. "O… here it is."
He raised his voice. "Uncle," he called. "I must come forth."

Gratiano's voice rang out from the hall:

"If thou attempt it, it will cost thee dear. Thou hast no weapon and perforce must suffer."

Othello smirked bitterly.

"Look in upon me, then, and speak with me. Or, naked as I am, I will assault thee."

Gratiano stepped through the door, sword drawn—but what he found was not an assassin. Just a man—barefoot, grief-slicked, and holding steel not like a killer, but like a pilgrim bearing his burden.

"What is the matter?"

Othello turned, raising the sword gently.

"Behold—I have a weapon. A better never did itself sustain upon a soldier's thigh…"

He looked down at the blade.

"I've seen the day that, with this little arm and this good sword, I made my way through more impediments than twenty times your stop…"

He paused. The sword lowered slightly.

"But… O vain boast."

He looked at the bed.

"Who can control his fate? 'Tis not so now…"

He stepped forward slowly, the sword now harmless in his grip.

"Be not afraid, though you see me weapon'd. Here is my journey's end… Here is my butt, my very sea-mark of my utmost sail."

He knelt beside Desdemona.

"Do you go back dismay'd? 'Tis a lost fear. Man but a rush against Othello's breast, and he retires. Where should Othello go?"

His voice broke.

"Now—how dost thou look now? O ill-starr'd wench!"

He touched her cheek.

"Pale as thy smock! When we shall meet at compt…"

His breath caught.

"This look of thine will hurl my soul from heaven… And fiends will snatch at it."

He kissed her brow, and the cold came off her like judgement.

"Cold… cold, my girl. Even like thy chastity…"

He rose, wild-eyed.

"O cursed slave!"

He lifted the sword again—not to strike, but to offer himself to vengeance.

"Whip me, ye devils! From the possession of this heavenly sight! Blow me about in winds! Roast me in sulphur! Wash me in steep-down gulfs of liquid fire!"

He fell once more beside her.

"O Desdemona! Desdemona! Dead! Oh! Oh! Oh!"

And just then—the door opened once more.

Lodovico entered, flanked by Montano. Behind them, Cassio—bloodied, broken—was carried in a chair. And among the guard, shackled, face like ironstone—Iago.

Lodovico scanned the chamber.

"Where is this rash and most unfortunate man?"

Othello raised a hand.

"That's he that was Othello," he said quietly. "Here I am."

Lodovico's eyes narrowed.

"Where is that viper? Bring the villain forth."

Othello turned. He looked down—toward Iago.

"I look down toward his feet…"

His voice changed. Grew quiet. Dangerous.

"But that's a fable. If thou be'st a devil…"

His hand tightened on the sword hilt.

"I cannot kill thee."

And with that, he struck.

Steel flashed—sank. The sword pierced Iago's side, sharp and swift, not wild, but judged. A wound meant to sting, not slay. Enough to leave Iago living… in ruin.

Iago gasped—bit back a cry—and staggered as the guards leapt forward.

"Wrench his sword from him!"

Lodovico barked.

Iago clutched his side, blood wetting his tunic.

"I bleed, sir," he said, with a grim smile. "But not kill'd."

Othello dropped the sword at last.

"I am not sorry neither. I'd have thee live… for in my sense, 'tis happiness to die."

He looked at Lodovico.

"O thou Othello," Lodovico said, sorrow heavy in his tone,
"Thou wert once so good…
Fall'n in the practice of a damned slave. What shall be said to thee?"

Othello raised his head.

"Why—anything. An honourable murderer, if you will. For nought I did in hate—but all in honour."

Lodovico turned to Iago.

"This wretch hath part confess'd his villainy. Did you and he consent in Cassio's death?"

Othello bowed his head.

"Ay."

The bodies lay like punctuation marks—full stops at the end of lives misspoken.

Cassio, carried in his chair, regarded the wreckage with heavy eyes.

"Dear general," he said gently, "I never gave you cause."

Othello—torn from his former self, gaunt and grey in soul—met his gaze.

"I do believe it," he said. "And I ask your pardon."

Then, turning to Lodovico, he gestured toward the shackled wretch, casting one final plea to the wreckage of justice.

"Will you, I pray, demand that demi-devil why he hath thus ensnared my soul and body?"

All eyes turned to Iago.

He stood apart, flanked by guards, manacled, his garments blood-streaked and torn. But it was not the mess of his hair or the sweat gleaming on his brow that marked the true change. No—what struck the room cold was that his very aspect had shifted. The mask was off. The mask had been the man.

Where once stood the witty ensign, the loyal ancient with a ready jest and twinkling eye, now hunched a creature more raw than reptile—his posture rigid and viperous. His once-charming eyes, so capable of mimicry and mirth, were now hard, black diamonds—reflecting only rage and an ancient, frozen contempt. His mouth, that clever shape-maker of lies, curled now into a wound. It was a sneer that grinned only downward—a scarlet fissure that mocked without mirth.

There was no remorse in him. None. He was the sort who would watch the world burn—just to warm his hands on its ashes. And though the play was ended and his deeds laid bare, still he looked victorious, as though this final ruin were always his design. That Desdemona was dead. That Othello lay broken. That Cassio limped. That Venice had been made to look a fool.

This was his empire.

He looked around at the room, measured the silence, and smiled—a smile not of glee, but of defiance. Then he spoke. Calmly. Silenced by his own truth, Iago had no more weapons. Like a defanged snake, all his venom had been in speech, in guise, in theatre. And now, exposed, unmasked, unmasked even to himself, there was simply… nothing left to say.

"Demand me nothing," he said. "What you know, you know. From this time forth, I never will speak word."

His silence was not retreat but extinction. He had spent his poison. His mouth, which once ruled the room, now hung empty. And just like that, the mouth—the final mask—was gone, sealed over. All that remained was the eyes. They watched, those eyes, cold as glass, souvenirs of a man long since emptied.

Lodovico stared at him in disgust.

"What? Not even to pray?"

Gratiano, hoarse from horror, answered for him.

"Torments will open your lips."

But Iago said nothing.

Othello only nodded.

"Well… thou dost best."

Lodovico turned, voice more formal now. "Sir, you shall understand what hath befall'n, which—as I think—you know not."

He produced a folded scrap.

"Here is a letter. Found in the pocket of the slain Roderigo."

He passed it to Cassio, who unfolded it slowly.

"And here another," Lodovico said, handing a second note. "This one imports the death of Cassio—to be undertaken by Roderigo."

Othello staggered.

"O villain!"

Cassio shook his head.

"Most heathenish and most gross!"

"And here's another," Lodovico added, "full of discontent. Roderigo meant to send it to this damned villain—"

He glared at Iago.

"—but belike, Iago came in the meantime… and satisfied him."

Othello clutched at the air like a drowning man.

"O the pernicious caitiff! How came you, Cassio, by that handkerchief—that was my wife's?"

Cassio spoke softly. "I found it in my chamber. And he himself—just now—confess'd he dropped it there… for a purpose."

Othello bowed his head.

"O fool… fool… fool."

Cassio continued, voice weighted with pity. "And in Roderigo's letter, he upbraids Iago—how he made him brave me on the watch. That's why I was cast. And even now, before dying, Roderigo said it plain: Iago hurt him. Iago set him on."

Lodovico raised his voice again, to the room and to history.

"You must forsake this room, and go with us. Your power and your command is taken off. Cassio rules in Cyprus."

He turned to Iago.

"As for this slave—if there be any cunning cruelty that can torment him much and hold him long, it shall be his. He shall lie close prisoner, till the nature of his fault be known to the Venetian state."

He made to leave.

"Come. Bring him away."

But Othello raised a hand.

"Soft you… a word or two before you go."

He turned to the assembled men, and to history itself.

"I have done the state some service," he said. "And they know't.
No more of that."

He stood straight, dignified not in defence—but in confession.

"I pray you, in your letters—when you shall these unlucky deeds
relate—speak of me as I am. Nothing extenuate. Nor set down aught
in malice."

He turned to Desdemona's bed.

"Then must you speak of one that loved not wisely, but too well. Of
one not easily jealous—but being wrought, perplex'd in the extreme.
Of one whose hand, like the base Indian, threw a pearl away— richer
than all his tribe."

His voice shook.

"Of one whose subdued eyes, albeit unused to the melting mood,
drop tears as fast as Arabian trees their medicinal gum."

He turned away from them all now, facing his end.

"Set you down this. And say besides…"

His voice dropped. Othello unsheathed the Spanish blade—Toledo
steel, fine as winter breath. He weighed it in his hand like memory,
then turned his face to the room and passed his sentence:

"…That in Aleppo once— Where a malignant and a turban'd Turk
beat a Venetian and traduced the state— I took by the throat the
circumcised dog, And smote him, thus."

He drove the blade into himself—not a frenzied stab, but a soldier's cut with the surety of one who has passed judgment: under the ribs, angled to the heart. The hilt struck flesh with a quiet, final thud. Blood rose instantly, black in the firelight, blooming through linen. He staggered once. Eyes wide, like the villain in his own story. Even his last words clung to the language of empire and othering, a soldier's comfort drawn from the savagery he once fought against.

Then turned to Desdemona.

"I kiss'd thee ere I kill'd thee..."

He bent, lips to hers. A farewell. A pardon.

"No way but this—killing myself, to die upon a kiss."

He fell. And did not rise.

Lodovico gasped. "O bloody period!"

Gratiano moved had forward—but too late.

"All that's spoke," he whispered, "is marr'd."

Cassio looked away.

"This did I fear," he said. "But thought he had no weapon. For he was... great of heart."

Lodovico turned to Iago.

"O Spartan dog..."

His voice was a curse.

"More fell than anguish, hunger, or the sea! Look on the tragic loading of this bed. This is thy work. The object poisons sight. Let it be hid."

He turned to Gratiano.

"You, keep the house. Seize upon the fortunes of the Moor—they fall to you."

He looked to Montano, to the guards.

"To you, Lord Governor, remains the censure of this hellish villain— the time, the place, the torture. O, enforce it!"

He stepped away, gathering his cloak.

"Myself will straight aboard. And to the state… this heavy act with heavy heart relate."

The room emptied. The door closed. The blood cooled. And silence returned. The great bed held them both—the general and his bride—united again, at last, in stillness. Around them, the wreckage of all that had moved and spoken and plotted. The final pieces of the game, scattered and unmourned. The candles guttered. Smoke coiled in the rafters like memory. Outside, the sea moved on without them. And somewhere far off, the bells of Venice tolled the hour. It was, perhaps, the farthest thing he had ever done from glory—and yet it was the most human. Not the act of a Moor, nor a general, nor a Venetian hero— but a man. Broken, betrayed, and made monstrous by love.

Thus fell Othello—lover, soldier, fool; a human being with a fragile heart of passion that turned green and broke. And thus, the curtain closed upon Cyprus, black as the blade that made it so.

EPILOGUE

In Which the Green-Eyed Monster Outlives Us All

There is a narrow street in Venice—one forgotten by maps but well remembered by shadows—where, on still nights, the walls seem to whisper. They do not speak of gondolas or lovers or lace, but of envy. Of a soldier who smiled and lied, and lied and smiled, until the smile broke and the lie remained. And though that street has changed names more than once, the tread of Iago's heel remains in the stone.

Centuries passed. Empires rose and rot. Languages changed. Theatres fell and were rebuilt. Venice grew quieter, her proud navy now moored for tourists and the ghosts. Yet the story endured, and one figure still walks undimmed among the rubble. He bears no scar. He needs no name. But he wears the mask of every age.

The story was retold in salons of the Enlightenment, where powdered minds debated: Was Iago a sociopath? An atheist? A genius of destruction? They drank Madeira and called him unknowable. Still he smiled. It was staged in theatres of velvet and gaslight, where actors twitched their moustaches and drew forth booming villainy, but missed the flicker behind the eyes. Still he smiled. In classrooms and lecture halls, he was dissected, pathologised, compared to Freud, to Machiavelli, to Milton's Satan—men searched for complexity like miners in a salt-flat. But Iago never needed to be deep. He only needed to be real.

And he was. For he was there in London too, years later, fog rising from the river. In the figure of a clerk who watched his brighter colleague rise while he remained invisible. In the heart of a housemaid who longed for the mistress's pearls, not for their worth, but for how they looked against skin. In a jealous husband. A scorned friend. A bitter child. He was there in every snub, every unvoiced wound that turned inward and festered until it needed a scapegoat. And he is here still. In offices, where promotion is passed like a secret handshake. In marriages, where old resentments hide in silences. On stages, screens, and scrolls. In the comment beneath a photo, the smirk behind a screen.

Iago does not wear his name. He wears yours. And mine. He is the man passed over. The friend unseen. The colleague who simmers. The lover who watches affection drift elsewhere. He is not brilliant. He is not mad. He is ordinary, and that is what makes him dangerous.

Let us then speak plainly. His motive, so long declared elusive, may not be elusive at all. It may be obvious. Too obvious for the lofty to admit.

Jealousy. A desire for what others possess. A hatred of the happy. A need to control, because one cannot create. He envied Othello's greatness. Desdemona's purity. Cassio's charm. Even Roderigo's foolish wealth. He envied them not for what they were, but for how they made him feel: small. And so he made them smaller, one by one, until he stood tall in the rubble.

And still he was not satisfied.

This is the monstrous simplicity of it: Iago was not a mastermind. He was a mirror. A man who saw what he lacked in others and turned love into ash to feel tall beside the ruin. His triumph, not grand, but bitter. He was not a devil. He was something worse. He was human.

And like mildew on the edge of a mirror, he waits still. In whispers. In glances. In the thought you have and quickly hide. That is where he lives now. Not on the stage. Not on the page. But behind your own reflection. And if we are honest, truly honest, we see the flicker of him in ourselves. Not slain. Not forgiven. Merely… among us.

So the tale ends, but not the telling. And somewhere, in the murmuring dark, the green-eyed monster still paces. Still watches. Still smiles.

Essays on Othello

Working with Charles

In some ways, it was much harder working with Charles, the Dickens model, than my other custom LLMs. This was because each iteration of him was utterly brilliant, even when they missed the mark. I often found myself breaking off the writing of the book in order to just bask in the banter with Dickensian flair. Iteration 1 was fantastic and, right at the get-go, it invented a wonderful cat in Act 1 Scene 1 that provided a hilarious percussion to Roderigo's plaintive mewling. That's my fancy of way of saying "bud-uhm-bum-pssht". As you can see, I've spent too long reading in the Dickens style! But by the time I was working on the definitive version of that scene, the final iteration kept messing up when I asked it to re-include said cat, and the blasted feline was set to steal the entire scene. So, I had to piece the different versions all together, and it was hard because the words were laid down so well, they fit together like a well-grouted mosaic, and I was loathe to prize bits up. With the Emily Bronte and Jane Ayre models, it was much easier to dismiss their lesser outputs, but Charles wrote everything brilliantly and then I was drowning in good versions. The problem was that Charles always swallowed Shakespeare and became Dickens, and that wasn't really what I wanted. I had to let it work only from the Shakespeare text if I wanted it to play nice, but foolishly I had already written the entire novel, TWICE, by the time I settled on the final process and config for the model. Yes, I wrote *Othello* twice, thought I was happy, went and wrote *Macbeth* (also written twice as it happens) and then came back and created the final iteration of— model, Charles. Then I used it to write the entire book again — Third time lucky, I suppose. Calibrating each of the LLMs for each book is really a matter of data and custom instructions. With the Emily Bronte model for *Macbeth The Gothic Novel*, there was only one novel in the training data of course (*Wuthering Heights*). The main difference is that training a model on all of Dickens' work means it has more data, and thus a much stronger voice. Emily Bronte's published works amount to around 120,000 words or so, Jane Austen a more respectable 700,000, but Charles Dickens wrote and published about 5 million words across his lifetime! And Dickens had such a wonderful and distinctive voice that it was a real pleasure to work with Charles, but so hard to edit it.

Because Charles was such a good writer, I decided to let his voice come through in some of the back matter essays here which touch on some of the timeless themes of *Othello*. Afterall, *Othello* was much more of a collaboration with the personality of this LLM than the other two books (*Macbeth* and *Romeo and Juliet*). As with each of the LLMs I used for the BARD409 series, this was a Socratic dialogue in terms of there being a lot of back and forth with the model. Re-writing and editing is what took the largest amount of time. So here are a few reflections on the process and the themes we tried to include.

Of Wokeness, Whiteness, and the War on Imagination

Obviously, one of the major themes to be explored in *Othello* is the issue of race and ethnicity. The play's inspiration was the Italian novella by Giraldi Cinthio in *Un Capitano Moro* ("A Moorish Captain"), a short tale of around 3,500 words published in 1565 as part of his *Hecatommithi* collection, in which the characters are unnamed and the plot is far simpler than Shakespeare's adaptation. This explains the Venetian setting, but also reflects how Renaissance novellas often used foreign or exotic figures as narrative devices rather than deeply human characters. Shakespeare likely read the story in Italian, as no English translation existed during his lifetime, further emphasizing his literary ambition and engagement with continental sources.

In recent years, a curious phenomenon has emerged: a vocal minority decrying the inclusion of diverse characters in period dramas and fantasy tales, citing "historical accuracy" as their rallying complaint. This lamentation often surfaces when a beloved story is reimagined with a cast that reflects the rich tapestry of our modern world. Yet, upon closer examination, these objections reveal more about the objectors than about the works they critique.

Consider the controversy surrounding diverse casting in recent period and fantasy adaptations. Productions like *Bridgerton* and *The Rings of Power* have faced online criticism for featuring racially diverse casts in settings often imagined as historically white. Critics have claimed such choices compromise "historical authenticity," despite the fact that both Regency England and medieval Europe were far more diverse than commonly portrayed. For instance, estimates suggest that up to 30,000 Black people lived in Britain during the Regency era, alongside a significant South Asian population, while medieval Europe saw Africans, Arabs, and diverse ethnic groups moving through port cities and royal courts. Even the 2017 live-action adaptation of *Beauty and the Beast*, a fairy tale set in a fictionalized 18th-century France where teapots sing and enchantresses roam, drew absurd complaints about casting choices—as though magical realism demands stricter racial demographics than historical reality. I would continue to refute these foolish online commentators, but as the Bard himself might say, "More of your conversation would infect my brain."

To demand rigid historical realism in stories that embrace fantasy, imagination, or selective historicism is to misunderstand both the genre and the history it loosely draws from. Fantasy worlds like Tolkien's Middle Earth, while inspired by medieval Europe, were never intended as exact replicas; and 18th-century France, far from being ethnically monolithic, was a hub of global trade, cultural exchange, and colonial interaction. Diverse casting in these contexts is not only defensible, but often more historically plausible than the sanitized, whitewashed versions of history that dominated earlier media. Ultimately, the outrage over inclusive casting reveals more about the biases of certain audiences than about any betrayal of historical truth.

Turning to Shakespeare's *Othello*, we encounter a narrative deeply rooted in its time yet remarkably resonant today. Othello, a Moorish general in the Venetian army, navigates a society rife with prejudice and intrigue. Some question the plausibility of a Moor attaining such a position in 16th-century Venice. However, historical records indicate that Venice, a hub of commerce and diplomacy, often employed foreign mercenaries and valued military prowess over lineage. The city was also home to numerous envoys, diplomats, and high-ranking officials from diverse cultures, reflecting its expansive trade networks and political reach across the Mediterranean and beyond. The character of Othello, therefore, is not a fantastical anomaly but a reflection of the complexities of Renaissance society.

In our novelization of *Othello*, we endeavoured to ground the narrative in the socio-political realities of the time. We explored the tensions between Venice and the Ottoman Empire, the strategic importance of Cyprus, and the intricate dynamics of race and power. While we preserved the original's raw exploration of jealousy and betrayal, we also sought to illuminate the systemic forces that shape the characters' fates.

Our adaptation does not shy away from the racial slurs and prejudices present in the original Shakespearean text. Instead, we present them within their historical context, allowing readers to grapple with the discomfort they evoke. Simultaneously, we highlight themes of feminism and autonomy, particularly through the characters of Desdemona and Emilia, whose strength and agency challenge the constraints of their society.

The insistence on "historical accuracy" often serves as a veneer for resistance to inclusivity. It is a selective invocation, rarely applied to the fantastical elements of a narrative but swiftly deployed when diversity enters the frame. Yet, history itself is a mosaic of cultures, identities, and experiences. To reflect this in our stories is not to distort the past but to honour its richness. In embracing diverse narratives and casting, we do not rewrite history; we reclaim it from the confines of a narrow lens. We acknowledge that imagination, like history, thrives on multiplicity. And in doing so, we invite all readers to see themselves within the tapestry of our shared human experience.

While debates about representation continue to shape our view of Shakespeare today, it's worth remembering that his original audiences approached his work with a very different mindset—seeking not so much political reflection, but lively entertainment.

Drinking Songs and Royal Performances:

Shakespeare's plays were meant to entertain, and it is easy to forget that they were enjoyed by both the masses and the monarchy. As such, they often contain allusions to the times that are easily lost on modern audiences. At first glance, the song Iago sings in Act II Scene 3 seems like a rough tavern ballad, and indeed it was a familiar song from the time. Yet beneath its alehouse swagger lies a shrewd commentary on pride, class, and kingship, perfectly attuned to the anxieties of a Jacobean audience. Line by line, the song exposes a subtle game: King Stephen is framed as a "worthy peer," but he quarrels about paying five shillings for a pair of trousers. He insults the tailor, calling him a "lown"—a scoundrel of low birth—and the repeated refrain urges humility: "Take thine auld cloak about thee." The apparent message is that pride, rather than poverty, leads to a kingdom's downfall.

Why place this in Iago's mouth? Because the song mirrors Iago's own tactics. He postures as an honest, plain-speaking soldier, while manipulating others' pride and ambition to their ruin. The surface lesson—that modesty is virtue—is undercut by Iago's actual behaviour. *Othello* is full of such inversions: appearances deceive, and virtue is often a mask for corruption. For the ruling monarch of the time, King James I, the song would have carried particular weight. James valued modesty and thrift (at least in theory) and had a keen eye for performances that reinforced moral virtue. In 1603, Shakespeare's company was officially renamed the King's Men, having received a royal patent from James himself—their first direct royal patronage. The King's Men were now expected to perform regularly at court as well as for public audiences, and Shakespeare, ever shrewd, tailored moments in his plays to flatter royal sensibilities without appearing overt. A familiar ballad warning against pride, tucked into the mouth of a villain, offered a kind of plausible deniability: it flattered James's ideals while also hinting at the dangers of false modesty and hidden corruption. Shakespeare's genius lies in his ability to balance entertainment with political acuity, crafting moments that could amuse, instruct, and gently warn, all without directly challenging the throne.

Importantly, the timing matters. *Othello* was first performed around 1603–1604, shortly after James ascended to the English throne. The mood was relatively stable; Shakespeare could be more playful in his handling of monarchy and pride. Even so, he disguises his commentary carefully, offering a theatrical sleight of hand that both flatters and warns the king.

In short, Iago's song is no random fragment. It is a sharp little emblem of the play's larger concerns: the danger of pride, the slipperiness of appearances, and the ease with which honour can be undermined from within. Through a bawdy drinking song, Shakespeare manages to weave a sophisticated commentary on personal ambition and political virtue—one that resonated with the common drinker and the crowned king alike. In the hands of the King's Men, performing for both crowded playhouses and the royal court, every jest and lyric became part of a larger dance: a performance that entertained, reassured, and occasionally, with a wink and a tune, held a mirror to power itself.

271

Othello and *Macbeth*: A Tale of Two Kingships

Alongside this adaptation of *Othello*, I have also written a novelisation of *Macbeth*—rendered in the darker, brooding style of Emily Brontë. While the two plays are close in date (*Othello* c.1603–1604; *Macbeth* 1606), the difference in tone between them is profound and revealing. *Othello* was performed at a time of relative optimism. James I had recently inherited the English crown, and there was a sense of cautious hope. Shakespeare could afford subtlety: he could weave criticisms into his plays, provided they were cloaked in irony and distance—such as giving a sharp song about pride to a villain like Iago. Audiences (and the king himself) could enjoy the play's wit without feeling personally attacked.

But everything changed with the Gunpowder Plot of 1605. The failed Catholic conspiracy to blow up Parliament and kill the king sent shockwaves through England. Fear of treason, paranoia about plots, and anxiety about rightful kingship became dominant. In this new climate, Shakespeare's tone shifts dramatically. *Macbeth*, first performed in 1606, is not playful. It is a grave meditation on ambition, guilt, regicide, and the fragility of the natural order. Shakespeare presents a cautionary tale: murder a king, and the heavens themselves will rebel. Macbeth's fall is swift and total, while the rightful bloodline (through Banquo's descendants) is prophesied to endure— pleasing news for a monarch like James, who claimed descent from Banquo.

In short: Where *Othello* teases, *Macbeth* repents. Where *Othello* masks its dangers with wit, *Macbeth* lays them bare in blood. Shakespeare, ever the astute observer of political weather, adjusted his plays accordingly. And it is within that sharp contrast that we see the full genius of his dramatic instinct—and the context that informs my adaptations. Less subtle is my plug for my other novelisation! Yet even as I explored crowns, conspiracies, and the raw machinery of power, another, more private theme stirred within *Othello*. Shakespeare's political flexibility—his ability to flatter kings while slyly questioning authority—finds its mirror in his own ambiguous sexuality, particularly his treatment of personal desire. Beneath the overt dramas of loyalty and betrayal lies a hidden current of obscure emotion, of intimacy that blurs the lines between friendship, loyalty, and love. In *Othello*, as in Shakespeare's own life and works, the boundaries are never clear—and it is within that ambiguity that some of the play's most unsettling power resides.

Fair Lord: Homoerotic Currents in *Othello*

When Charles and I reached the boiling point of *Othello*'s Act III Scene III—the infamous dream speech—I found myself pausing. Something about it had always unsettled me: not just the scene's rawness, but the charge that lay unspoken in the air between Iago and Othello. I instructed Charles:

> *"I want to push the homoeroticism here. It's already there, isn't it? Lying just beneath the surface."*

Charles agreed immediately, calling it "criminally underexplored." I wouldn't call it that necessarily, as there is a growing body of scholarship on this issue. In his 1931 book, Ernest Jones—the early psychoanalytic critic and student of Freud— famously proposed that Iago's motives could not be reduced to ambition or jealousy alone, but also contained a submerged, unspoken erotic drive. In Jones's reading, Iago's hatred of Othello masks a deeper attraction, twisted into malice. Jonathan Crewe, in his chapter "Queer Iago: A Brief History" (2018), traces Iago's diagnosis as a latent homosexual across multiple sources, though critiquing the older ones for their essentialisation of Iago as an "*ipso facto* woman-hating male homosexual." More recent scholars, including Anthony Guy Patricia in *Queering the Shakespeare Film* (2017), and Bruce R. Smith in *Homosexual Desire in Shakespeare's England* (1991), have expanded this view, tracing a broader current of homoerotic tension across Shakespeare's works.

Shakespeare's plays are rich with these blurred lines of affection, desire, and betrayal. His *Sonnets*—particularly the *Fair Youth* sequence—are addressed not to a woman, but to a beautiful young man. The language of those sonnets is intimate, jealous, and deeply charged. Shakespeare's own sexuality remains a matter of scholarly debate, but few serious critics now deny that homoeroticism is stitched through his work. Figures like Stephen Orgel, Mario DiGangi, and Jonathan Goldberg have all contributed to a growing body of scholarship that resists any simplistic or heteronormative reading of his texts.

In Shakespeare's original playtext, this scene cries out for physical interpretation. Iago's retelling of Cassio's dream is vivid, bodily, and laced with suggestion: gripping, wringing hands, hard kisses, legs thrown over thighs. Stage productions have often picked up on this, adapting it either for dark comedy or to amplify the scene's destabilising homoerotic power. But when Charles first drafted our novelisation of the moment, it was too restrained. It treated Iago's story like a report—a dry recounting—without letting the full sensual, unsettling atmosphere breathe. I pushed for a revision. In the final version, Iago doesn't simply *tell* the story: he *embodies* it. He mimes Cassio's grip, he brushes his own lips, he almost whispers the kisses into Othello's face. His body becomes part of the lie. His performance is not just evidence; it is seduction, calculated to infect Othello's imagination with shame and jealousy at once.

Of course, we needed to ground it. Iago's "I lay with Cassio lately" line carries an implicit intimacy, but historically, men often shared beds out of necessity, especially soldiers. Cyprus, after the battle and the great storm, would have offered few comforts—half the barracks ruined, men crammed into what dry space remained. Charles and I agreed to weave this context lightly into the narration: enough to make sense of the sleeping arrangement, without neutralising the scene's dangerous ambiguity. We refined the moment further by having Iago address Othello as "my Fair Lord"—a deliberate echo of Shakespeare's own diction in the Sonnets. "Fair youth," "fair friend," "fair lord"—the language of courtly, male-to-male affection runs throughout Shakespeare's work. Inserting it here not only anchors the scene within that tradition, but also twists it: the compliment becomes a provocation, a suggestion of past or possible intimacy that Othello cannot bear to consider. We briefly toyed with slipping in a direct quotation from Sonnet 20—"A man in hue, all hues in his controlling"—but ultimately decided against it. Better, we thought, to let the spirit of Shakespeare's sonnets haunt the prose without drawing obvious attention. The careful reader will feel the resonance.

Our goal was never to impose modern interpretations onto Shakespeare. Rather, by amplifying the homoerotic tension already latent in the scene, we reveal just how sophisticated—and subversive—his handling of human desire really was. Shakespeare rarely offers clean motives or straightforward passions. He preferred the dangerous, shifting ground where love, envy, lust, and hatred bleed into one another. In the end, we let the scene speak with its own uncomfortable honesty. "Fair Lord" falls from Iago's lips not as a sneer, but as a poisoned caress. Othello recoils, not only from jealousy, but from a deep, visceral sense of taint—his own world of honour,

273

masculinity, and marriage suddenly fouled by images he cannot unsee. And attentive readers—those who know the Sonnets, those who sense the darker music playing beneath the play's surface—will know exactly what has been loosed.

Soft Power and Hard Truths: Feminism, Desdemona, and Emilia in *Othello*

Interestingly, despite the themes of race and homoeroticism that surfaced as we worked on Othello, one of the major themes that took a lot of care and re-working pertained to feminism and the role of the women in the play. As Charles and I worked through the novelisation of *Othello*, there came a moment — midway through Act III — when I found myself getting increasingly irritated with Desdemona.

"Is she being thick?" I asked Charles, as Desdemona continually goes on about Cassio in the face of Othello's rage. She even says his crime was almost nothing, even though he stabbed Montano, the former governor of Cyprus at a time of great political sensitivity. It was a half-joking reaction, but the frustration was genuine and familiar to many modern readers. Desdemona's repeated pleas on Cassio's behalf, her refusal to read the gathering storm around her, begin to chafe. She seems bafflingly naive, even as the noose tightens. This irritation sparked a larger question for me: How do we handle Shakespeare's women — particularly Desdemona — when adapting them for a modern, psychological novel? Not by crudely modernising them, or by crowbarring slogans into the text (although as I will detail later, I did sneak in some Margaret Attwood), but by listening carefully to what Shakespeare hinted at and drawing those threads into fuller life.

Desdemona, as Shakespeare wrote her, was not built for psychological realism. She is an emblem: of loyalty, virtue, and tragic blindness. In the early acts, she shines with self-assurance, choosing Othello against her father's wishes, speaking boldly before the Venetian court. But by Act III, she becomes something else: not a living character, but a symbol. Her goodness hardens into obtuseness. Her trust in words — her belief that love and reason can persuade — leaves her fatally exposed to a world that runs not on persuasion, but on pride, violence, and honour. Many productions and readers have wrestled with this shift. Directors have tried to reinvigorate her; feminist critics have pointed out the structural cruelty of her role. And as I adapted the novel, I knew I could not simply leave her as Shakespeare left her, luminous, but helpless. Instead, I tried to reveal the emotional realism beneath the tragedy. Desdemona is not a fool. She is a young woman raised to believe that virtue is persuasive, that goodness is armour, that love can tame men. She steps into the masculine world of the military — Cyprus, garrisoned and raw after battle — with those ideals intact, and never realises they are doomed, until she sees it on the face of her beloved.

Her feminism, if we can call it that, is implicit: a faith in the power of speech, of mercy, of reasoned love. It is tragic, not triumphant. She believes she can change things with words, but discovers too late that she cannot even save herself. In this reading, her death is not just pitiable, it is inevitable. Set against her is Emilia: a woman who has lived long enough to know the rules. From the start, Emilia is all instinct and wariness. She loves Desdemona and there is no cynicism in her affections, but she also sees the world as it is, not as it ought to be. Where Desdemona pleads, Emilia endures. Where Desdemona believes, Emilia doubts. And where Desdemona is shattered by betrayal, Emilia is already walking wounded. That is until, at last, she finds the courage to name injustice aloud, and pays for it with her life.

In the novel, I tried to let Emilia breathe fully: not as a heroine, not as a caricature, but as a woman who has survived too much to be deceived anymore. The brief flashes — her knowingness in the garden, her tired banter with Iago, her handling of the handkerchief — all build toward her final, shattering moment of truth. She is the counterpoint Desdemona needs. and, in a grim way, her mirror.

Feminist scholarship has long recognized these tensions. Critics like Marilyn French (*Shakespeare's Division of Experience*, 1981) and Carol Thomas Neely (*Women and Men in Othello*, 1980) have pointed out that Othello's women are trapped in a patriarchal system they can neither fully understand nor escape. However, later critics, such as Ruth Vanita have complicated this view, emphasizing that Shakespeare's women are not merely victims but active agents navigating a brutal world. Elizabeth Massie has emphasized that the women of *Othello* are burdened by the crushing expectations of Venetian—and by extension Elizabethan—ideology, where obedience is seen as 'natural' and resistance is punished as 'unnatural.' Desdemona represents idealism crushed under masculine violence; Emilia represents survival scorched into bitterness. Bianca, too often dismissed, signals how even those on the margins are policed and blamed. None of these women are simple, and none are safe. Together, they sketch a tragic map of how power constrains even the most spirited hearts.

In adapting the novel, I drew on these readings, not by hammering them home with anachronistic dialogue, but by letting them rise naturally through the characters' actions, silences, and growing unease. In the end, Desdemona and Emilia are not failures of Shakespeare's imagination. They are two tragic possibilities, two ways women live, love, and die under systems designed to silence them. Feminism in *Othello* is not about rebellion as much as it is about recognition. And that, perhaps, is why their deaths still strike so bitterly true.

Erased Spaces: Feminist Shadows in Desdemona's Fall

As we reworked the pivotal confrontation between Desdemona and Othello — the moment when love first darkens into threat — I found myself pushing for a deeper seam of feminism to run beneath the prose. Shakespeare, in the original, already gives Desdemona glimpses of fear. When she asks Othello, "What horrible fancy's this?", it's not a challenge but a tremor. She senses the shift from romance to danger but she cannot yet name it. I wanted to go further. In our novel, I pushed for this to become the moment Desdemona's *naivety dies*.

Here, in his penetrating stare, she sees the lover who wooed her with tales of wonder replaced by the soldier, the veteran of twenty campaigns, the man who could burn cities and call it duty. His gaze is not furious but disciplined, cold. It is the gaze of a man who, if convinced of righteousness, could destroy without hesitation, even her. This became the emotional pivot of the scene. It was at this point I suggested we thread in the feminist insight of Margaret Atwood, who wrote:

> *"Men are afraid that women will laugh at them. Women are afraid that men will kill them."*

That unspoken truth needed to live inside Desdemona's realisation. Without anachronism, we let it hum beneath her breath. There is no need to spell it out further. It lives in the white space between her whispered words. But we didn't stop with Atwood. As we shaped the narration around Desdemona's growing dread, we layered in a quiet echo of Judith Butler — whose *Gender Trouble* reminds us that womanhood is not essence but performance, stylised and scripted by a rigid cultural frame. Thus, Desdemona becomes trapped not merely in her marriage, but in a wider structure of perception. She is no longer speaking to Othello the man — she is speaking to the role he now sees her playing: seductress, traitor, enemy. Her actual words no longer matter. The script is already written. We wove this awareness into the prose with care, drawing on Atwood again for atmosphere:

> *She was trapped in one of those blank white spaces at the edge of the world,*
> *not waiting to be spoken for, but to be patterned over.*

This line lets the spectres of Atwood, Butler, and even Charlotte Perkins Gilman (with her visions of women dissolving into wallpaper patterns) breathe inside the text — without ever announcing their presence. A reader attuned to feminist literature will hear the resonance. Others will feel it instinctively, as Desdemona does. The result, I hope, is a Desdemona who does not simply blunder into her death. She crosses a threshold: from innocence to knowledge, from hope to horror. She sees — for the first time — that love does not always protect. That men are not always what they seem. And that a woman, even loved, may still be erased.

Shrouded in White: The Willow Song and the Meaning of the Wedding Sheets

When we reworked Desdemona's final scenes, one symbolic thread became crucial: the wedding sheets she asks Emilia to lay on her bed — and, if need be, to wrap her body in when she dies. Historically, wedding sheets in early modern Europe were not just bedding, they were proof. On the wedding night, a bloodstain upon the sheets was taken as public evidence of a bride's virginity; a visible, physical sign that she had fulfilled her role. In noble families, these sheets were sometimes shown to witnesses, folded and kept as part of a marriage's honour, binding not just individuals but dynasties. No stain, no proof. No proof, no honour.

In Shakespeare's *Othello*, this silent pressure hums beneath Desdemona's request. She is not merely preparing her bed, she is preparing her *evidence*, her *defence*, her *shroud*. Without fully knowing it, she is trying to protect herself the only way she can: by clinging to the outward signs of purity, even as the world around her turns to suspicion and death. In our novel, we drew this thread tighter. Desdemona's folding of the wedding sheets becomes an act of fatal innocence. She believes virtue is a shield, that love will protect her, and that her traditional bloodstained proof will save her. But the truth is already clear: no sheet, no evidence, no argument will change what Othello has decided to see. Set alongside the Willow Song — the old ballad of female abandonment and sorrow — the symbolism sharpens. Desdemona is not simply grieving love; she is performing her own ritual death, enacting the final tragedy of a woman who trusted the symbols of loyalty more than the shifting realities of power. In the novel, when Desdemona sings and folds the wedding sheets, it is no longer merely sad. It is horrific in its inevitability; the silent preparation of a woman who does not yet know that her innocence has already been reinterpreted, already erased. And so the Willow and the white sheets — song and cloth — become her twin laments: One sung aloud. One stitched in silence.

The Monster Iago: On Motive and Jealousy

There's a long and tangled tradition of scholars trying to explain Iago's motives. Dr Johnson thought Iago was simply evil for evil's sake. Coleridge famously called it "motiveless malignity" — the idea that Iago acts out of pure, inexplicable wickedness, a sort of human embodiment of chaos. Others have pointed to sexual jealousy, racism, ambition, wounded pride. A whole symphony of possible causes. And yet, when Charles and I were working on the novel, it seemed simpler than all that. The answer, I thought, was right there in the text. Iago warns Othello about jealousy, calling it "the green-eyed monster which doth mock the meat it feeds on." But he is describing himself.

Iago is jealous. Of Cassio's easy grace. Of Desdemona's affection. Of Othello's power, his marriage, his myth. Iago envies, resents, and hungers to destroy — not for strategy, but for satisfaction. He is the green-eyed monster he pretends to warn against. That's why, in our version, we let that thread rise to the surface in the final Dickensian epilogue, giving readers a glimpse of the simple, bitter truth at the heart of all Iago's chaos. Not motiveless malignity. Not deep psychological complexity. Just jealousy, pure and corrosive. Sometimes, Shakespeare doesn't hide the answer. Sometimes he whispers it, plain enough, if you're willing to listen.

Conclusion

Writing and reimagining Othello has been, more than anything, a pleasure. It's a play that gripped me from the first time I read it at school. I was lucky enough to see it live in Shakespeare's birth-town of Stratford-upon-Avon on a school trip, though my favourite version is the 1995 film adaptation, largely due to Kenneth Brannagh's Iago. I myself am an old-fashioned person (or a snotty one), and so I carry a handkerchief most days — unless, like Bilbo Baggins, I rush out on some last-minute adventure and forget it. But I have learned a few things since school: I never give handkerchiefs as gifts, and I try, wherever possible, not to allow the monster of jealousy to mock me. It rarely ends well. In order to avoid jealously, one must learn to be at peace in the present moment, and I'm a little jealous of anyone who can manage that.

Thank you for supporting independent publishing

10% of the profits from this book will be donated to ecological and literacy charities. We believe in giving back, encouraging reading, and helping make technology more sustainable for our planet.

If you enjoyed this book, check out the rest of the **BARD409** series, where Shakespeare's plays are reimagined in the voices of other great authors. You can sign up for updates, bonus content, and new releases at *www.hungrywolf.net*.

About the Author

Richard S. Pinner is a writer and applied linguist based in Tokyo. His work explores the intersections of language, literature, and technology. His previous books include *Moloch: A Collection of Poems Made with the Interference of Computers* and *Augmented Communication: The Effect of Digital Devices on Face-to-Face Interactions* (Palgrave Macmillan). His debut novel, *The Bad Boys in the Attic*, was written during COVID lockdown and is available from Hungry Wolf Press. When not writing, he teaches, travels, and takes his dog on long walks in the park.

Find him at *www.rspinner.net*.

www.ingramcontent.com/pod-product-compliance
Lightning Source LLC
Chambersburg PA
CBHW061949170626
46813CB00006B/2583